'Are we going somewhere?' Esme asked.

'Yes, we're returning to the royal palace,' Zaid said.

'Why do I feel that there's more going on here than you're telling me?' she pressed.

A muscle rippled in his jaw. 'Because there is. I suggested that we take some time to absorb the possibility that you may be carrying my child. I was wrong to do so. If you are truly carrying my child, then we need to put certain arrangements in place.'

'What kind of arrangements?' she asked suspiciously.

'The kind that you will be apprised of in due course.'

'So I will be the last to know?'

'No, you will be one of the first to know when final decisions have been made.'

She wasn't going to get any more out of him.

Esme became blindingly aware of one thing. Whether her pregnancy had been confirmed or not didn't matter to Zaid. While his heir was even a possibility he was going all out to lay his claim on it.

Maya Blake's hopes of becoming a writer were born when she picked up her first romance at thirteen. Little did she know her dream would come true! Does she still pinch herself every now and then to make sure it's not a dream? Yes, she does! Feel free to pinch her, too, via Twitter, Facebook or Goodreads! Happy reading!

Books by Maya Blake

Mills & Boon Modern Romance

Pregnant at Acosta's Demand
Signed Over to Santino
A Diamond Deal with the Greek
Married for the Prince's Convenience
Innocent in His Diamonds

One Night With Consequences
The Boss's Nine-Month Negotiation

Rival Brothers
A Deal with Alejandro
One Night with Gael

The Billionaire's Legacy
The Di Sione Secret Baby

Secret Heirs of Billionaires
Brunetti's Secret Son

Seven Sexy Sins
A Marriage Fit for a Sinner

Visit the Author Profile page
at millsandboon.co.uk for more titles.

THE SULTAN
DEMANDS
HIS HEIR

BY
MAYA BLAKE

MILLS & BOON

First Published in Great Britain 2017
By Mills & Boon, an imprint of HarperCollins*Publishers*
1 London Bridge Street, London, SE1 9GF

© 2017 Maya Blake

ISBN: 978-0-263-07005-7

MIX
Paper from
responsible sources
FSC® C007454

This book is produced from independently certified FSC paper
to ensure responsible forest management. For more information
visit www.harpercollins.co.uk/green.

Printed and bound in Great Britain
by CPI Group (UK) Ltd, Croydon, CR0 4YY

THE SULTAN
DEMANDS
HIS HEIR

CHAPTER ONE

ESME SCOTT JERKED awake in the split second between her phone vibrating and the bell ringtone blaring through her darkened bedroom. Heart racing, she lifted her head off the pillow and stared at the illuminated screen.

As a social worker, it wasn't unusual for her phone to ring in the middle of the night. The problems of her wards and an overstrained system required twenty-four-hour dedication.

Except she knew instinctively that *this* phone call had nothing to do with her job. The same gut instinct she'd been forced to hone for less altruistic purposes in her past.

But she'd left that life far behind.

After the fourth ring, she reached for the phone, willing her hand to stop shaking.

'Hello?'

'Am I speaking to Esmeralda Scott?'

Esmeralda. Her heart sank further. The only person who used her full name was her father. The man she hadn't spoken to or seen in eight long years.

She forced her jaw to relax. 'Y-yes.'

'Daughter of Jeffrey Scott?' came the deep, cultured, slightly accented query. The voice was stamped with enough authority and arrogance to make her grip tighten on the handset.

No, this was no ordinary phone call.

Sitting up, she turned on her bedside lamp, although she couldn't focus on anything but the ominous voice on the line.

'Yes. Who is this?'

'My name is Zaid Al-Ameen. I'm the chief prosecutor

in the Royal Kingdom of Ja'ahr.' The voice was filled with deep pride. Implacable purpose.

Esme's breath snagged in her lungs, but she refused to let the premonition lurking in her mind take hold. 'What can I do for you?' she asked, using the tone she reserved for calming her most agitated wards.

Momentary silence met her cool query. 'I called to inform you that your father is in jail. He's due to be arraigned in two days when formal charges will be brought against him.'

A thousand icicles pierced her skin, the boulder in her stomach confirming that even though she'd written him off when she'd walked away eight years ago, her father still possessed the power to rock her foundations.

'I...see.'

'He insisted on using his one phone call to reach you, but it seems the number he had for you is out of order.'

There was speculation in the crisp, no-nonsense tone but Esme wasn't prepared to inform him that she'd made sure her number was unlisted for this sole purpose.

'So how did *you* find me?' she asked, her mind swirling with a thousand questions. None of which she wanted to air to the deep-voiced stranger on the phone.

'I have one of the best police forces in the world, Miss Scott,' he replied haughtily.

I?

The possessive reply made her frown a little, but she couldn't put off the one question sitting on the tip of her tongue no matter how much she hated to ask. 'What are the charges against him?'

'They're too long to list. Our investigation unearths a new charge almost on the hour,' he replied, his voice growing colder with every answer. 'But the main charge is fraud.'

Her heart banged harder against her ribs. 'Right.'

'You don't seem surprised by the news.' This time the query held stronger speculation that snapped her spine straight.

'It's the middle of the night here in England, Mr. Al-Ameen. You'll pardon me if I'm struggling to take it all in,' she replied, transferring the phone to her other hand when her palm grew clammy.

'I'm aware of the time difference, Miss Scott. And while we're not under obligation to track you down on behalf of your father, I thought you might like to know about the incident—'

'What incident?' she blurted.

'There was an altercation in the jail where your father is being held—'

'Is he hurt?' she demanded, her stomach hollowing at the thought.

'The medical exam shows a mild concussion and a few bruises. He should be well enough to be returned to custody tomorrow.'

'So he can be attacked again or will you be doing something to protect him?' she screeched, tossing aside the duvet to get out of bed. She paced from one end of her small bedsit to the other before the man at the end of the phone deigned to answer.

'You father is a criminal, Miss Scott. He doesn't deserve special treatment and he will be given none. Consider yourself fortunate to be receiving this courtesy call at all. As I mentioned before, his arraignment is in two days. It's up to you to attend if you wish. Goodnight—'

'Wait! Please,' she added when the man didn't hang up. Esme forced herself to think rationally. Were this one of her young wards, what would she do?

'Does he have a counsel? I'm assuming he's entitled to one?'

The terse silence that greeted her told her she'd caused

offence. 'We're not a backward country, Miss Scott, despite what the world's media likes to portray. Your father's assets are frozen, as is the law in fraud cases, but he's been given a public defender.'

Esme's heart sank. In her experience, most public defenders were overstretched and overworked. Add the fact that her father was indubitably guilty of the charges levelled against him and the outlook was bleak.

The part of her that experienced the urge to end the conversation right now and pretend this wasn't happening was immediately drowned out by the heavy guilt that followed. But she'd cut ties with her father for a very good reason. She'd turned her life around. She wouldn't feel guilty for that.

'Can I talk to him?'

For several seconds, silence greeted her request. 'Very well. Provided he's given the all clear by the doctors, I'll allow him to make one more phone call. Make yourself available at six a.m. Goodnight, Miss Scott.'

The line disconnected, taking the authoritative voice with it.

A tiny knot in her stomach, caused solely by that charged, electric quality to her caller's voice, unfurled. She dropped the phone and returned to sit on her bed, her vision blurring as her hands shook. As Zaid Al-Ameen had loftily stated, Esme wasn't surprised by the news. If anything, she was only surprised it had taken eight years to finally arrive.

She exhaled roughly, willing the guilt and anger and pain to subside. When after a full ten minutes she still hadn't managed to wrestle her emotions under control, she rose and padded to the small desk in the corner of her bedroom.

Further sleep tonight was out of the question. The only way to prevent the vault of bad memories straining to crack open was to fill her time with work. Her work, which thankfully involved concentrating on other people's problems rather than her own, always managed to distract her. From the very first day she'd stepped into her junior social worker role four years ago, she'd welcomed that distraction simply because her actions produced positive results. Sometimes in indistinguishable ways, other times more meaningfully. Either way was good enough, although not good enough to ever wipe away the black stain on her soul.

Touch Global Foundation, the worldwide foundation she worked for, dealt directly with local organisations to help the disadvantaged, with numerous arms offering everything from drug rehabilitation to residential relocation.

Except working now, with her father's news fresh in her mind, was near impossible. Esme forced herself to finish up the notes recommending rehousing for a single mother of four to a better neighbourhood, and a dyslexia test for the second child. She set a reminder to follow up her recommendation with a phone call, and closed the file.

Calling up her search engine, she typed in the relevant information. Although during the frenzied pockets of time she'd spent with her father he'd often talked of the Kingdom of Ja'ahr, they'd never visited that country. It hadn't been on *the list*. Back then, decadent, well-established kingdoms like Monaco and Dubai and the brighter lights of New York and Vegas had been more desirable.

Within minutes, Esme understood why her father had taken an interest in Ja'ahr. The small kingdom, poised on the edge of the Persian Gulf, had gained as much international renown as its well-known neighbours in the last decade for all the right reasons.

Clever brokering of its rich resources of oil, gems and shipping lanes had seen it attain world's richest status, catapulting its ruler and royalty to extreme wealth, while the lower classes had been left far behind. Such a divide wasn't uncommon in such countries, but in Ja'ahr's case it was staggering.

Inevitably, the result of such a divide had caused political and economical unrest, some of which had escalated into violence. *All* of which had been ruthlessly suppressed.

Esme cautioned herself not to believe everything she read on the Internet. But disturbing stories about the Kingdom of Ja'ahr's judicial system were hard to dismiss. Stiff sentences were handed down for the lightest of offences, with even more ruthless punishment meted out to re-offenders.

'We're not a backward country, Miss Scott, despite what the world's media likes to portray.'

Except their judicial system seemed backward. Right back to the Dark Ages. Which didn't bode well for her father.

He deserves it. Remember why you walked away?

Jaw clenching, she straightened her spine.

She'd walked away. *She'd* changed her life for the better.

The reminder bolstered her up until her phone rang. Resolutely, she answered.

'Hello?'

'Esmeralda? Is that you?'

Her free hand tightened into a fist, her eyes closing at the deep, familiar voice.

'Yes, Dad, it's me.'

His exhalation was tinged with relief. Followed by a rough laugh. 'When they told me they'd actually managed to reach you I thought they were having me on.'

Esme didn't answer. She was too busy containing the cocktail of emotions that always swirled inside her when it came to her father.

'Baby girl, are you there?' Jeffrey Scott asked.

The endearment was so bitter-sweet, she didn't know

whether to laugh or cry. 'I'm here,' she managed after a minute.

'Okay, I guess you know what's happened?'

'Yes.' She cleared her throat, hoping her mind would follow suit. 'Are you all right? I was told you had concussion.'

Her father laughed, but the sound lacked its usual bravado. 'A concussion is the least of my worries. Not if the big man gets his way.'

'The big man?'

'Yes. The Royal Punisher himself.'

She frowned. 'I'm sorry, Dad. What are you talking about?'

'The chief prosecutor is gunning for me, Esmeralda. I've already been denied bail. And he's putting in a petition to fast-track my trial.'

The memory of the deep, powerful voice on the phone momentarily distracted her, made her breath catch a little. Then her hand tightened on the phone. 'But you have a lawyer, don't you?'

The laughter was starker. 'If you call a lawyer who told me my case was hopeless and advised me to plead guilty and save everyone the trouble a proper defender.'

Despite what she'd read about Ja'ahr's judicial system, she was still shocked. 'What?'

'I need you here, Esmeralda.'

This time her breath stayed locked in her throat. Along with the inner voice that screamed a horrified *No*.

When she'd tossed around scenarios of how she would conduct this reconnection with her father, she hadn't deluded herself into thinking he wouldn't want something from her. Money had been the most likely bet since his assets were frozen. She'd even mentally totted up her savings, and girded her loins to part with some of it.

But what he was asking of her...

'I've done a little research. They're very big on character witnesses over here during trials,' he continued hurriedly. 'I've put you down as mine.'

Déjà vu whispered down her spine. Wasn't this how it had always started? Her father innocently asking her to do something? And her guilt eating away at her until she obliged?

Esme stiffened, reminding herself of that last, indefensible thing he'd done. 'Dad, I don't think—'

'It could make the difference between me dying in prison or returning home one day. Will you deny me that?'

Esme firmed her lips. Remained silent.

'According to my lawyer, The Butcher is going for life without parole.'

Her heart lurched. 'Dad…'

'I know we didn't part on the best of terms, but do you hate me that much?' her father asked, after another long stretch of silence.

'No, I don't hate you.'

'So you'll come?' He latched on hopefully, his voice slipping into the oh-so-familiar smooth cajoling that even the hardest heart couldn't resist.

She closed her eyes. Reminded herself that in the end she *had* resisted. She'd been strong enough to walk away from him. But, of course, that didn't matter now.

Because no matter what had gone on before, Jeffrey Scott was the only family she had. She couldn't leave him to the mercy of a man known as The Butcher.

'Yes. I'll come.'

The relief in her father's voice was almost palpable, but the torrent of gratifying words that followed washed over Esme's head as she contemplated the commitment she'd just made. Eventually she murmured her goodbyes as her father's allotted time ended their call.

Almost detached, she typed another name into the

search engine. And forgot the ability to breathe as she stared into the brandy-coloured eyes of The Butcher.

The formidable authority in those eyes was just the start of the shockingly arresting features of the chief prosecutor of the Kingdom of Ja'ahr. She already knew what his voice sounded like. Now she saw how accurately it matched the square, masculine jaw that could have been cut from granite. It was shadowed despite the clean shave and, coupled with sharp cheekbones resting on either side of a strong, haughty nose, slightly flared in suppressed aggression, it was near impossible to look away.

Blue-black hair sprang back from his forehead in short, gleaming waves, the same colour gracing winged eyebrows and sooty eyelashes. But what captured her attention for a breathless moment was the sensual lines of his mouth. Although set in grim purpose in the picture, she couldn't help but be absorbed by them, even wonder if they ever softened in a smile or in pleasure. Whether they would feel as velvety as they looked in pixels.

The alarming direction of her thoughts prompted a hurried repositioning of the mouse. But that only revealed more of the man whose magnetism, even on screen, was hypnotising. Broad shoulders and a thick neck were barely restrained in the dark pinstriped suit, pristine shirt and immaculate tie he wore. Long arms braced an open-legged stance, displaying a towering figure with a streamlined body that had been honed to perfection.

He stood before a polished silver sign displaying the name of a firm of US attorneys. Esme felt a tiny fizz of relief at the thought that she'd got the wrong hit on her search. But clicking the next link revealed the same man.

Only he wasn't the same. His compelling features and hawk-like stare were made even more compelling by the traditional garb draping him from head to toe. The *thawb* was a blinding white with black and gold trim, repeated in the *keffiyeh* that framed his head and face.

With deep trepidation, Esme clicked one last link. Her gasp echoed in her bedroom as she read the biography of the thirty-three-year-old man nicknamed The Butcher.

Only the man who'd disturbed her sleep last night with bad news wasn't just the feared chief prosecutor of an oil-rich kingdom. He was so much more. Gut clenching, her gaze drifted back up to the mercilessly implacable face of Zaid Al-Ameen. Sultan and Ruler of the Kingdom of Ja'ahr.

The man who held her father's shaky fate in his hands.

CHAPTER TWO

ZAID AL-AMEEN RESTED his head against the back seat of the tinted-windowed SUV transporting him from the court-house. Only for a moment. Because a moment was all he had. His caseload was staggering. A dozen cases waited in the briefcase on the seat next to him, with dozens more waiting in the wings.

But even that was secondary to the colossal weight of his responsibilities as ruler of Ja'ahr. A weight that made each day feel like a year as he battled to right the wrongs of his uncle, the previous King.

A fair number of his ruling council had been shocked by his intention to carry on with his chosen profession when he'd returned from exile to take the throne eighteen months ago.

Some had cited a possible conflict of interest, questioning his ability to be both an able ruler *and* a dedicated prosecutor. Zaid had quashed every objection by doing what he did best—following the letter of the law and winning where it counted. Meting out swift justice had been the quickest way to begin uprooting the rank corruption that had permeated Ja'ahr's society. From the oil fields in the north to the shipping port in the south, no corporate entity had been left untouched by his public investigative team. Inevitably, that had made him enemies. Khalid Al-Ameen's twenty-year corrupt rule had birthed and fed fat cats who'd fought to hold onto their power.

But in the last six months things had finally started to change. The majority of factions that had strenuously opposed and doubted him—after all, he was an Al-Ameen like his late uncle—had begun to ally with him. But those unused to his zero tolerance approach still incited protestors against him.

His bitterness that his uncle had escaped Zaid's personal justice by falling dead from a heart attack had dissipated with time. It was an outcome he couldn't change. What he could change was the abject misery that his people had been forced to endure by Khalid.

Zaid had first-hand, albeit deadly experience of the misery crime and the greedy grasp for power could wreak. That he'd lived through the experience was a miracle in itself. Or so the whispers went. Only Zaid knew what had happened that fateful night his parents had perished. And it was no miracle but a simple act of self-preservation.

One that had triggered equal amounts of guilt, anger and bitterness over the years. It was what had driven him to practise law and pursue justice with unyielding fervour.

It was what would bring his people out of the darkness they'd been thrust into.

Lost in the jagged memories of his past, it took the slowing of the lead vehicle in his motorcade to alert him to his surroundings.

A large group of protestors was gathered in a nearby park normally used to host summer plays and concerts. Some had spilled into the street in front of his motorcade. Protests weren't uncommon, and, although regretful, it was part of the democratic process.

Zaid glanced around him as a handful of his personal security began to push back the crowd.

Ja'ahr City was particularly magnificent in early April, new blooms and moderate weather bathing the city in sparkling beauty. Giant sculptures and stunning monuments, surrounded by verdant gardens containing exotic flowers, lined the ten-mile-long central highway that led from the courthouse to the palace.

Except, as with everything else, this particular display

of Ja'ahr's wealth had been carefully cultivated to fool the
world. One only had to stray along a few streets on either
side of the highway to be met with the true state of affairs.

The grim reminder of the wide chasm dividing the social classes in his kingdom forced his attention back to the
crowd and the giant screen showing a reporter surrounded
by a handful of protestors.

'Can you tell us why you're here today?' the female
journalist asked, thrusting her microphone forward.

The camera swung toward the interviewee.

Zaid wasn't exactly sure why his hand clenched on his
thigh at the sight of the woman. In the previous life he'd
led in the United States, he'd had numerous liaisons with
women more beautiful than the one currently projected on
the super-sized screen in the park.

There was nothing extraordinary about her individ-
ual features or the honey blonde hair tied in a bun at her
nape. And yet the combination of full lips, pert nose and
wide green-grey eyes was so striking his fingers moved,
almost of their own accord, to the button that lowered his
window. But still he couldn't decipher what had triggered
the faint zap of electricity that had charged through him
at the sight of her. Perhaps it was the determined thrust of
her jaw. Or the righteous indignation that sparked from
her almond-shaped eyes.

Most likely it was the words falling from her mouth.
Condemning. Inciting words wrapped in a husky bedroom
voice and amplified on speakers that threatened to distract
him even as he strained to focus on them.

A voice he'd heard before, slightly sleep husky, over
the phone in the middle of the night. A voice that had,
disturbingly and inappropriately, tugged at the most masculine part of him.

'My father has been attacked twice in prison during
the last week, while under the supervision of the police.

Once was bad enough, considering he suffered a concussion then. But he was attacked again today, and I'm sorry, but twice is not acceptable.'

'Are you saying that you hold the authorities responsible?' the reporter prompted.

The woman shrugged, causing Zaid's gaze to drop momentarily from her face to the sleek lines of her neck and shoulders, her light short-sleeved top clearly delineating her delicate bones and the swell of her breasts. He forced his attention up in time to hear her answer.

'I was given the impression that the authorities here are practically the best in the world, and yet they can't seem to keep the people under their care safe. On top of that, it seems I won't be allowed to see my father until his trial or until I offer a financial incentive to do so.'

The reporter's eyes gleamed as she latched onto the delicious morsel. 'You were asked for a bribe before you could see your father?'

The woman hesitated for a millisecond before she shrugged again. 'Not in so many words, but it wasn't hard to read between the lines.'

'So I take it your impression of Ja'ahr government so far isn't a good one?'

A sardonic smile lifted her mouth. 'That's an understatement.'

'If you could say anything to those in charge, what would you say?'

She looked directly into the camera, her wide eyes gleaming with purpose. 'That I'm not impressed. And not just with the police. These people here clearly believe that too. I believe a fish rots from the head down.'

The reporter's gaze grew a touch wary. 'Are you alleging that Sultan Al-Ameen is directly culpable for what happened to your father?'

The woman hesitated, her plump lower lip momentarily disappearing between her teeth before emerging, gleaming, to be pressed into a displeased line. 'It's apparent that something's wrong with the system. And since he's the one in charge, I guess my question to him is what's he doing about the situation?' she challenged.

Zaid hit the button, blocking out the rest of the interview just as his intercom buzzed.

'Your Highness, a thousand apologies for you having to witness that.' The voice of his chief advisor, travelling in the SUV behind him, was almost obsequious. 'I have just contacted the head of the TV studio. We are taking steps to have the broadcast shut down immediately—'

'You will do no such thing,' Zaid interjected grimly.

'But, Your Highness, we can't let such blatant views be aired—'

'We can and we will. Ja'ahr is supposed to be a country that champions freedom of speech. Anyone who attempts to stand in the way of that will answer directly to me. Is that clear?'

'Of course, Your Highness,' his advisor agreed promptly.

As his motorcade passed the last of the protestors, he caught one last, brief glimpse of the woman on a much closer screen. Her head was tilted, the sunlight slanting over her cheekbone throwing her face into clear, more captivating lines. His jaw tightened at the further sizzle of electricity, until he was sure it would crack.

'Do you wish me to find out who she is, Your Highness?'

He didn't need to. He knew exactly who she was.

Esmeralda Scott.

Daughter of the criminal he intended to prosecute and put behind bars in the very near future. 'That won't be necessary. But have her brought to me immediately,' he instructed.

As he hung up, he allowed the inner voice to question why he was going out of his way to trigger such a knee-jerk reaction. A second later, he smashed it away.

The why wasn't so important. What mattered was her maligning the fragile pillars of the very things he was fighting to restore in his country. Integrity. Honour. Accountability.

Esmeralda Scott needed to answer a few questions of her own. After which he would take pleasure in pointing out the errors of her ways to her.

Esme gave in to the frantic urge to slide her clammy palms down her skirt as the black town car with tinted windows sped her towards an unknown destination. She'd cautioned herself a dozen times against letting fear take over. So far it hadn't.

Perhaps it had something to do with the bespectacled, harmless-looking man sitting across from her and his re-assurance that her interview had gained her the right audience on behalf of her father.

'Where are we going?' she asked for the second time, her mind still spinning at the swiftness at which her appearance on TV had earned her attention.

The question earned her a slightly less warm smile. 'You will see for yourself when we arrive in a few minutes.'

The fear she'd staunched looming a little larger, Esme glanced out the window.

She began to notice that the landscape was growing more opulent, the parks even greener and studded with staggeringly beautiful works of art. Why that triggered a stronger sense of trepidation, Esme wasn't sure. Sweat that had been steadily beading the back of her neck, despite the air-conditioning of the car, rolled between her shoulders.

'My father's prison hospital is on the other side of the city,' she attempted again.

'I am aware of that, Miss Scott.'

Alarm trickled through her. 'You never said how come you knew my name.' She'd only given the journalist her first name during the interview.

'No, I did not.'

She opened her mouth to press for a clearer answer but closed it again as the car swerved in a wide circle before approaching huge double gates painted in stunning gold leaf. They slowed long enough for armed guards to wave them through.

'This…is the Royal Palace,' she mumbled, unable to stop her voice from shaking as she stared at the immense azure-coloured dome that could rival St. Peter's Basilica in Rome.

'Indeed,' the man responded, not without a small ounce of relish.

The town car drew to a firm stop. The sweat between her shoulders grew icy. She cast another, frantic glance outside.

The penny finally dropped. She was here, at the Royal Palace. After publicly calling out the ruler of the kingdom.

Dear God, what have I done?

'I'm here because of what I said on TV about the Sultan, aren't I?'

A sharply dressed valet opened the door and the chief advisor stepped out. He signalled to someone out of sight before he glanced down at her. 'That is not for me to answer. His Highness has requested your presence. I do not advise keeping him waiting.'

Before she could answer, he walked away, his shoes and those of his minders clicking precisely on the white and gold polished stone tiles that led to the entrance steps of the palace.

Esme debated remaining in the car as alarm flared into full-blown panic. The driver was still seated behind the wheel. She could ask him to take her back to her hotel. Even beg if necessary. Or she could get out and start walking. But even as the thoughts tumbled she knew it was futile.

Another set of footsteps approached the car. Esme held her breath as a man dressed in dark gold traditional clothes paused beside the open door and gave a shallow bow. He, too, was flanked by two guards.

They seem to travel in threes.

She was tossing away the mildly hysterical observation when he spoke. 'Miss Scott, I am Fawzi Suleiman, His Royal Highness's private secretary. If you would come with me, please?'

The question was couched in cultured diplomacy, but she had very little doubt that it was a command.

'Do I have a choice?' she asked anyway, half hoping for a response in the affirmative.

The response never came. What she witnessed instead was the firmer, watchful stance of the bodyguards, even while Fawzi Suleiman bowed again and swept out his arm in a polite but firm *this-way* gesture.

Esme alighted into dazzling sunshine and a dry breeze. She took a moment to tug down her knee-length black pencil skirt and resisted the urge to adjust her neckline. Fidgeting was a sign of weakness, and she had a feeling she would need every piece of her armour in place.

Slowly, she raised her chin and smiled. 'Lead the way.'

He took her words literally, walking several steps ahead of her as they entered the world-famous Ja'ahr Palace.

At first sight of the interior her steps slowed and her jaw dropped.

Tiered Moorish arches framed in black lacquer and gold leaf veered off half a dozen hallways, all of which converged in a stunning atrium centred by a large azure-tiled fountain.

She dragged her gaze away long enough to see that they'd arrived at the bottom of wide, magnificent, sweeping stairs. Carpeted in the same azure tone that seemed to be the royal colour, the painstakingly carved designs that graced the bannisters were exquisite and grand.

Truly fit for a king.

A faintly cleared throat reprimanded her for dawdling. But as they traversed hallway after hallway, past elegantly dressed palace staff who surreptitiously eyed her, awe gave way to a much more elemental emotion.

She'd been expertly manipulated. With clever words and non-answers, but tricked nevertheless. Esme could only think of one reason why.

Intimidation.

They arrived before a set of carved double doors. She curbed the panic that flared anew, clutching her purse tighter as Fawzi Suleiman turned to her.

'You will wait here until you're summoned. And when you enter, you will address the Sultan as *Your Highness*.'

He didn't wait for her response, merely grasped the thick handles and pushed the doors wide open.

'Miss Scott is here, Your Highness,' she heard him murmur.

Whatever response he received had him executing another bow before turning to her. 'You may go in.'

She'd taken two steps into the room when she heard the doors shut ominously behind her. Despite the slow burn of anger in her belly, Esme swallowed, fresh nerves jangling as the faint scent of incense and expensive aftershave hit her nostrils.

She was in the presence of the ruler of Ja'ahr.

She forced her feet to move over the thick, expensive Persian rugs she was certain cost more than she would earn in two lifetimes as she emerged into the largest personal office she'd ever seen. Esme's entire focus immediately zeroed in on the man behind the massive antique desk.

From the photos on the Internet she'd known he was a big man. But the flesh and blood version, the larger-than-life presence watching her in golden-eyed silence, was so shockingly visceral, she stumbled. She caught herself quickly, silently admonishing herself for the blunder.

A dozen feet from his desk, his magnetic aura hit her, hard and jolting. She wanted to stop walking but she forced herself to take another step. And then she froze as he rose to his feet.

It was like being hit with a tidal wave of raw masculinity. At five feet five, she considered herself of average height but her heels added a confidence-bolstering three inches. None of that mattered now as she took in the towering man looking down his domineering royal nose at her.

He was dressed in a three-piece suit, but he may as well have been adorned in an ancient warrior's suit of armour, such was the primitive air of aggression Zaid Al-Ameen gave off as he watched her. Above his head, a giant emblem depicting his royal kingdom's coat of arms hung, emphasising the glory and authority of its ruler.

But even without the trappings of all-encompassing wealth and power, Esme would have been foolish to underestimate the might of the man before her.

She summoned every last ounce of composure. 'I... don't know why I've been brought here. I haven't done anything wrong. Your Highness,' she tagged on after a taut second.

He didn't respond. Esme forced herself to return his intense stare as she fought the urge to wet her dry lips.

'And I hope you don't expect me to bow. I'm not sure I can do it correctly.'

One imperious brow lifted. 'How would you know unless you try?' he drawled.

A spike of something hot and unnerving shot through her midriff at the sound of his accented voice. Deep, gravel rough, filled with power, it rumbled like ominous thunder. Esme's shiver coursed down to her toes.

'It may be the done thing, but I don't think I want to.'

An enigmatic expression crossed his face, disappearing before she could accurately decipher it. '"But I don't think I want to, *Your Highness*".'

She blinked, dragging her attention from his exotically captivating face. 'What?'

'You were told of the correct form of address, were you not? Or does your lack of respect for my country and my judicial system extend to my station as well?'

The throb of anger in his voice sent a chill over her nape. She was in the lion's den, faced with its incredibly displeased occupant. Regardless of her personal feelings, she needed to tread carefully if she wanted to escape with her hide intact.

'My apologies, Your Highness. I didn't mean to cause offence.'

'How is it possible that I've known of your existence only a short time and yet I'm ready to add *insincere* to the list of your unsavoury attributes?'

Her mouth gaped. *'Excuse me?'*

'Excuse me, *Your Highness*.' This time the command was coated in ice, his eyes reflecting the same frigid displeasure as he regarded her.

Esme attempted to curb the angry words tripping over her tongue. She failed. 'Perhaps it has something to do with being brought here against my will. *Your Highness*.'

With measured strides, he rounded his desk. Esme

couldn't help but stare. Despite his immense size, he moved like poetry in motion. Like a stealthy predator, focused on only one goal.

Vanquishing his prey.

CHAPTER THREE

ESME EXPECTED A cataclysmic event to occur in the seconds it took for him to prowl closer. Such was the power of the force field he wielded. Instead, Zaid Al-Ameen stopped a few feet from her, his gaze capturing hers as a frown pleated his brow.

'You were brought here against your will?'

'Well...yes. Somewhat. Your Highness.'

'The answer is either yes or no. Did my men lay their hands on you?' he enquired, his voice a touch rougher.

She had to lock her knees to keep from doing something stupid. Like crumbling into an inelegant heap at his feet. Because the closer he got, the higher she craned her neck, the more her brain scrambled. 'I...er...'

'Were you harmed in any way, Miss Scott?' he demanded in a near growl.

'No...but your emissary misrepresented himself.'

He stopped moving, his eyes narrowing. 'How?'

'He didn't tell me he was bringing me here for a start. He gave me the impression that he was taking me to my father—'

'But no one touched you?'

Esme couldn't understand why he was so hung up on that. But she shook her head. 'No one touched me, but that doesn't alter the fact that this is a form of kidnapping.'

He clasped his hands behind his back, but that didn't diffuse the power of his presence. If anything, his focus sharpened on her face, his eyes raking her from temple to chin and back again. 'You weren't told that I wished to speak to you?'

'Not until we got here. And I got the feeling that I wouldn't be allowed to leave even if I wanted to.'

He remained silent for a moment, hawk-like eyes probing her every breath. 'First you allege that the authorities wanted a bribe in order for you to see your father, and now you're alleging a potential kidnapping, even though you came here of your own free will. Are you in the habit of making assumptions about everything, Miss Scott? Or getting into the vehicles of men you think wish you harm?' The accusation was delivered in a low, pithy tone as he took yet another step closer.

The icy fingers crawling up her back shrieked at her to retreat from the wall of bristling manhood coming at her. But Esme had learned to stand her ground a long time ago.

So, even though her instinct warned that Sultan Zaid Al-Ameen posed a different sort of danger from that she was used to, perhaps an even more potent kind, she angled her chin and stubbornly met his gaze. 'No, Your Highness. I'm in the habit of judging a situation for myself. But if I'm wrong, here's your chance to prove it. I wish to leave,' she threw out.

That left brow arched again. 'You just got here.'

'And as I said, Your Highness, I thought I was being taken to see my father and not…'

'Not?'

'Bundled here for…whatever reason you've had me brought here. I'm assuming you're going to tell me?'

'In due course.'

Her response stuck in her throat as he strode past her. The mingled trail of incense, aftershave and man that sneaked into her senses momentarily distracted her. Esme found herself turning after him, her feet magnetically taking a step in his direction.

'Come and sit down,' Zaid Al-Ameen said.

The invitation was low and even, but another layer of apprehension dragged over her skin. She glanced at the closed doors through which she'd walked a few minutes ago.

'Just for the hell of it, if I said no, that I want to leave, will you let me?'

'You may leave if you wish to. But not until we've had a conversation. Sit down, Miss Scott.' There was no mistaking the command this time, or the inference that she wouldn't be allowed to leave until he was ready to let her go.

Esme gripped her purse tighter, her fingers screaming with the pressure on the leather. Pulse tripping over itself, she followed him to the sitting area and perched on the nearest seat.

Almost on cue, the doors opened and his private secretary appeared, bearing a large, beautifully carved tray of refreshments.

He set it down, executed another bow, then waited with his hands clasped respectfully in front of him.

Zaid Al-Ameen sat down in the adjacent seat and looked at her. 'Do you prefer tea or coffee?' he asked.

About to refuse because she didn't think she could get anything down her throat, she paused, keenly aware of the two sets of eyes watching her.

'Tea, please, thank you. Your Highness,' she hastily added after a sharp look from Fawzi.

His master cast her a sardonic look before nodding to Fawzi, who moved forward and prepared the tea with smooth efficiency.

Bemused, Esme accepted the beverage, almost afraid to handle the exquisite bone china. She refused the delicious-looking exotic treats Fawzi offered her, then waited as Sultan Al-Ameen's coffee was prepared and handed to him.

Fawzi bowed again and left the room.

Silence reigned as Esme took another sip, and attempted to drag her gaze from the slim, elegant fingers gripping his coffee cup. After taking a large sip, he set the cup back on the saucer and swung his penetrative gaze to her.

'Contrary to what you wish me to think, you know exactly why you're here.'

The muscles in her belly quivered, but she fought to keep her voice even. 'My television interview in the park?'

'Precisely,' he intoned.

Sensing the beginning of a tremble in her hand, she gripped her cup harder. 'I thought Ja'ahr advocated free speech among its citizens?'

'Free speech is one thing, Miss Scott. Skirting the inner edges of slander is another matter entirely.'

The quivering in her belly escalated. *'Slander?'*

'Yes. Disrespecting the royal throne is a criminal offence here in Ja'ahr. One that is currently punishable by a prison sentence.'

'Currently?'

'Until that law, like a few others, is amended, yes. Perhaps that is what you wish? To be tossed in prison so you can keep your father company?' Zaid Al-Ameen enquired in a clipped tone.

'Of course it isn't. I only wanted… I was frustrated. And worried for my father.'

'So you always leave your common sense behind when your emotions get the better of you? Are you aware that some of the allegations you made this afternoon are serious enough to put you in danger?'

The rattle of the cup had her hastily setting it down. 'Danger from who?'

'For starters, the police commissioner doesn't like his organisation or his reputation questioned so publicly. He could bring charges against you. Or worse.'

Fear climbed into her throat. 'What does *worse* mean?'

'It means you should've given your words a little more thought before you went on live television.'

'But…everything I said was true,' she argued, unwilling to let fear take over.

His lips pursed for a moment. 'It would've been prudent to take into account that you're no longer in England. That things are done somewhat differently here.'

'What does that mean?' she asked again.

He discarded his own cup and saucer then leaned forward, his arms braced on his knees. The action caused his wide shoulders to strain beneath his suit, drawing her unwilling attention to the untamed power beneath the clothes.

A hint of it emerged in a low rumble as he spoke. 'It means my magnanimity and position are the only things keeping you out of jail right now, Miss Scott, given the fact that some of the allegations you claim to be true are unfounded.'

'Which ones?'

'You said your father was attacked twice in the last week. But my preliminary investigation tells a different story.'

Her breath caught. 'You've looked into it already?'

'You maligned my government and me on live television,' he replied in icy condemnation. '"The fish rots from the head" I believe were your exact words? I don't take kindly to such an accusation, neither do I leave it unanswered.'

She felt a little light-headed. 'Your Highness, it...wasn't personal—'

'Spare me the false contrition. It was a direct challenge and you know it. One I took up. Quite apart from my intimate knowledge of your father's many crimes, do you want to know what else I discovered?'

The taunting relish in his voice told her she didn't. But she swallowed down the *No* that rose in her throat. 'You're going to tell me anyway, so go ahead.'

'I have it on good authority, and on prison security footage, that your father instigated both confrontations. He seems to be under some misguided delusion that his fate will be less dire if he's seen as a victim.'

She tensed as the words struck a little too close to the bone. Jeffrey Scott was a master at reading situations and adapting to them. It was the reason he'd survived this long in his chosen profession.

Eagle eyes caught her reaction. 'I see you're not surprised. Neither are you hurrying to his defence,' he observed. 'Perhaps some of what I've said rings truer for you than the picture you painted of him on live TV?'

She took a deep, steadying breath. No matter what she knew in her heart, she wouldn't incriminate her father by answering the question. 'That doesn't alter the fact that the guards didn't take action after the first incident,' she replied. 'Perhaps if he'd been released on bail—'

'So he could attempt to take the first flight out of the country? Your father is a veteran con man, which, judging by your continued lack of surprise, is not news to you. And yet he's named you as his principal character witness,' he mused, his eyes cutting into her.

'As the man prosecuting my father, isn't it unethical to discuss the case with me, Your Highness?' she parried.

His grim twist of his lips told her he'd seen through her evasion tactics. 'Nothing I've said so far contravenes the correct judicial process, Miss Scott. You can trust me on that.'

His biographer had called him a master tactician, able to mould the word of law like putty in his hands, but never breaking it. Esme needed to proceed with caution if she didn't want to be tripped up. 'Did you bring me here to point out the error of my ways before you throw me in jail, too?'

'I brought you here to warn you against indulging in any further public outbursts. If you wish to exhibit any more rash decision-making, wait until you're back home in England.'

Affronted heat crawled up her neck. 'That sounds distinctly like a threat, Your Highness.'

'If that's what it takes to get through to you, then so be it. But know that you're treading on extremely thin ice. I won't tolerate any further unfounded aspersions cast against me or my people without solid proof to back them up. Is that understood?'

The sense of affront lingered, attempting to override the same tiny voice she'd ignored during her interview. This time it urged her to be thankful that she wasn't being hauled over royal coals. She was struggling with the dissenting emotions when, taking her silence as assent, he rose.

His towering frame made her feel even more insignificant, so she scrambled to her feet. Only to lose her balance as one heel twisted beneath her. She pitched forward, a gasp ripping from her throat as her hands splayed in alarm.

Strong hands caught her upper arms at the same moment she dropped her purse and her open hands landed on his hard-muscled chest. She heard his sharp intake of breath and felt her own breath snag in her lungs as heat from his body almost singed her palms.

Esme's head snapped up, that compulsion to look into those eyes once again a command she couldn't ignore. His eyes had darkened, the light brandy shade now a burnished bronze that fused incisively with hers. This close, she saw the tiny gold flecks that flared within the darker depths, the combination so mesmeric she couldn't look away, despite the frisson shooting up her arm. Despite the lack of oxygen to her brain from the breath she couldn't take.

Despite the fact that she shouldn't be touching him, this man who was hell-bent on exerting his supreme authority over her. Who was hell-bent on keeping her father in prison.

Move!

Her palm started to curl, in anticipation, she told herself, of pushing back from him. But the infinitesimal tightening of his fingers stopped her. Absorbed by the gleam in his eyes, by his scent swirling around her, Esme remained immobile. His nostrils flared slightly as his gaze dropped to her mouth. Almost as if he'd touched them, her lips pulsed with an alien sensation that absurdly felt like excitement. Hunger.

She didn't...*couldn't* want to kiss him, surely?

He released her so suddenly she wondered if she'd spoken the thought aloud. Spoken it only to have it promptly, ruthlessly rejected.

She stepped back, silently urging her legs not to let her down, even as another wave of heat swept over her face.

She needed to leave. Now.

As if the same thought had struck him, Zaid Al-Ameen turned abruptly and walked away, his imposing figure carrying him to his desk. Released from the trap of his puzzling, spellbinding presence, she sucked in a much-needed breath then snatched up her purse. She straightened to the sound of him issuing a rasped instruction into his intercom. Seconds later, the door reopened.

His private secretary barely glanced her way, his attention focused solely on the Sultan and the rapid words of lyrical Arabic falling from his lips. Esme was so distracted by the exotic, melodic sound that she didn't realise they'd stopped speaking and were staring at her until the silence echoed loudly in the room.

For the third time in a disgracefully short period her face heated up again. 'I'm sorry, did you say something?' she addressed Fawzi, unwilling to catch another mocking glance from Sultan Al-Ameen.

The private secretary looked a little perturbed at being addressed directly in the presence of his master. He stood straighter. 'His Highness said you are free to go. I am to escort you to your chauffeur.'

Knowing it would be impolite to leave without acknowledging him, Esme reluctantly redirected her gaze to the Sultan. 'I... I'm...'

One sardonic brow elevated, the look he sent her haughty enough to freeze water. 'You pick a curious time to become tongue-tied, considering your desire to leave has been granted. The next time we meet will be in the courtroom when you testify on behalf of your father. Let us hope you're not as inarticulate under cross-examination. I would hate to see all the effort you made to come to the aid of your father wasted. Goodbye, Miss Scott.'

The dismissal was as final as the drive back to the hotel was quick. Even after she was safely back in her hotel room, Esme still couldn't force her heartbeat to slow. She'd been summoned, judged and found severely wanting.

And yet the righteous anger she'd felt in Zaid Al-Ameen's presence was no longer present. Instead, awareness from his touch clung to her skin, her mind supplying an alarmingly detailed play-by-play of the moment he'd stopped her from falling. With each meticulous recounting her body grew hot and tight, her breathing altering into shameful little pants that drew a grimace of disgust at herself. To distract her out-of-control hormones, Esme turned on the TV and channel-surfed, only to come face to face with herself in a replay of her interview. Forcing herself to watch, she experienced a twinge of remorse as her words echoed harsh and condemning in the room.

The stone of unease in her belly hadn't abated hours later when she was in bed, attempting to toss and turn herself into sleep. Sleep came reluctantly, along with jagged, disturbing dreams featuring a breathtakingly hypnotic figure with brandy-coloured eyes.

The intensity of the dream was so sharp, so vivid she jerked awake.

Only to find it was no dream. There was someone in her room.

Esme's breath strangled in her lungs as she battled paralysing fear and scrambled upright. The dark, robed figure outlined ominously against her lighter curtains tensed for a watchful second then launched after her the moment she scurried off the bed. Her feet tangled in the sheets, ripping a cry from her throat. She sensed rather than saw the figure rounding the bed towards her as she pushed at the sheets and crawled away on her hands and knees. A few steps from the bathroom she attempted to stand.

A strong, unyielding arm banded her waist, plastering her from shoulder to thigh against a hard, masculine body. He lifted her off the floor with shocking ease, her feet kicking uselessly as he evaded her efforts to free herself. Acute terror finally freeing her vocal cords, Esme screamed.

The large hand that clamped over her mouth immediately muffled the sound.

Terrified by the ease with which the intruder had caught and restrained her, Esme fought harder. She wrapped her fingers around the thick wrist and was attempting to pry him off when she felt his warm breath against her cheek.

'Calm yourself, Miss Scott. It is I, Zaid Al-Ameen. If you wish to remain safe, you need to come with me. Right now.'

CHAPTER FOUR

ESME SLACKENED IN shock for a handful of seconds before outrage kicked in. At her renewed struggle, he held her tighter. 'Be calm,' he commanded again.

She shook her head, her heart tripping over all the possible reasons for his presence here in her room, holding her prisoner. She came up with nothing remotely reassuring. 'You have my word that I mean you no harm, Esmeralda. But I need your reassurance that you won't scream before I release you,' he said, his lips brushing against her ear.

Despite her racing heart, she felt herself go still. She told herself it wasn't the effect of the deep but lyrical lilt to her first name as it fell from his lips, or the low, even way he spoke that finally soothed her, but the need to be set free from the deeply disturbing sensation of the body welded to hers.

No longer fighting, she was keenly aware of the firm strength of his body against hers. The splay of the fingers of his restraining arm branding her hips. Her bare legs dangling against his longer ones. Her back absorbing his unhurried breathing as her bottom snuggled between the widened stance of his hips. And the highly masculine, very proud organ cradled between them.

Heat surging up her body, Esme jerked her head in quick assent. He waited a beat then released her. She launched herself away from him, slapped her hand on the light switch in the bathroom before whirling to face him.

The sight of the Sultan of Ja'ahr, dressed from head to toe in black traditional clothes, every inch the dark desert warrior lord he was, threatened to rob her of the breath she'd just regained. The hand she lifted to push back her

heavy hair shook as she glared at him. 'You may be the
ruler of this kingdom, but you have no right to invade my
privacy,' she condemned, a touch too shakily. 'Not to mention the fact that you scared the living—'

One imperious hand slashed through the air. 'I understand that you wish to express your outrage. But I highly
recommend you do so once we're away from the hotel.'

'Why?' she demanded.

Not bothering to dignify her with a response, he strode
to the small wardrobe on the other side of the room. Esme
watched, stunned, as he began to rummage through her
clothes.

'What on earth do you think you're doing? If you think
I'm going anywhere with you after barging into my room
in the middle of the night, think again.'

He turned from the wardrobe, his eyes narrowed in
displeased slits. 'I caution you against using that tone of
voice with me or my men will arrest you, with or without
my permission.'

Her eyes widened. 'Your men?'

He jerked a head towards the door. Esme followed his
action and for the first time she noticed the men who stood
guard, their broad backs to the door but rigidly alert. Protecting their King.

Barring her way.

'Why are they here? Why are *you* here?'

He stepped forward and she saw that he held her black
cotton dress in his hand. 'I don't have time to debate the
matter with you. Put this on. We need to leave now, unless you plan on walking out of the hotel dressed in that
wispy scrap of nothing?' he rasped. Although his expression remained stoically impersonal, his voice was a touch
more raw than before.

Esme stared down at the peach night slip she wore.
The silky, lace-edged material was short, barely coming

to mid-thigh. The bodice consisted of two cupped trian-
gles also edged in lace, with thin straps joining at her nape
in a halter design. As nightwear went, it was intended to
be feminine and sexy, hugging, flattering and titivating
where necessary.

Except, with Zaid Al-Ameen's piercing gaze on her,
Esme bypassed those middling sensations and went
straight to fiery hot awareness between one heartbeat and
the next. Mild shock rippled through her belly at the intensity of the feeling singeing her body as his gaze conducted a slow journey over her. When it rose from her feet
to linger at her thighs, a heavy throbbing commenced between her legs. The sensation rippled outward, sparking
tiny fireworks that exploded beneath her skin as it spread.

Dark golden eyes rose higher, over her stomach to rest
on her breasts. Suddenly sensitive peaks prickled, then
slowly tightened into hard nubs. Realising that the silk
exhibited every reaction of her body, Esme hastily threw
her arm up over her chest, even as she defied the hot flush
staining her neck and cheeks to stare challengingly at him.

But she might as well have been a gnat challenging an
elephant. The eyes that met hers may have been a touch
more turbulent than they were moments ago, perhaps even
gleaming with a hint of suppressed hunger, but the man
who strode determinedly over to her and thrust her dress
at her was once again the supreme marauder intent on
having his way.

'You have two minutes to put this dress on or I will do
it for you myself,' he pronounced succinctly.

Even though she caught the dress, Esme stood her
ground. 'I'll put the dress on, but I'm not leaving this
room until you tell me what is going on.'

At his curt nod, she stepped back into the bathroom and
shut the door firmly behind her. About to put the dress on,
she froze when she caught sight of her reflection in the

mirror. Her long loose hair was in complete disarray, her colour high as her chest rose and fell in agitation. But it was the brightness of her eyes that shocked her most of all. Where she'd expected fear, she read something else. Something that made her skin tingle even more wildly. Her nipples were still tight twin points of blatant arousal and belatedly she realised that, standing in the light of the doorway, Sultan Zaid would have been able to see right through her slip.

With renewed chagrin and heightened disquiet, she turned away and tugged the dress over the night slip. There was no way she was going back in there to retrieve her bra so the nightgown would have to offer the extra protection she needed. Besides, she could feel Sultan Zaid's restless prowling through the bathroom door.

After sliding her fingers through her hair in a vain effort to control the unruly mess, she tugged it into a ponytail and left the bathroom to confront the figure pacing the room. 'Okay, I deserve to know what's going on, and I'm not moving until I do.'

'The chief of police is on his way to arrest you. And unless you come with me, you will be in jail within the hour. It won't be a pleasant experience.'

Her mouth dropped opened, but the stark words had shrivelled her vocal cords and killed any further protest in her throat. Her gaze swung to the guards standing at the door. They hadn't moved, but she sensed an escalated urgency in the air.

He'd turned on a lamp while she'd been in the bathroom and Esme hurried across the room to shove her feet into the heels she'd discarded at the bottom of the bed. Then she went to the wardrobe and tugged out her suitcase. It was ripped from her hand a second later.

'What do you think you're doing?' he demanded.

'I'm getting my things.'

'There's no time for that. Your belongings will be taken care of.'

Again she wanted to protest, but at the implacable look in his eyes she nodded. Her purse held her passport, credit cards and phone. He waited long enough for her to grab it before he marched her to the door.

Eight bodyguards immediately positioned themselves in a protective cordon around them. A lift she suspected had been held especially for him transported them swiftly to the ground floor.

They exited to a large, empty foyer with only a sleepy male receptionist stationed behind the desk. He straightened to attention, then bowed respectfully as they moved past him.

Sultan Zaid barely glanced at him, his focus on the revolving doors. And the small group of armed men walking through it.

Her heart leapt into her throat. Beside her, Zaid tensed, even though he didn't break his stride.

'Remain by my side and do not speak.' The words were delivered in a low, even voice, but the stern command that pulsed through them was unmistakeable.

She nodded as the small group drew closer. Their posture and uniforms announced who they were before she read the insignia on their attire.

The leader, a small, rotund man, came forward and in unison they executed a bow, but she noted that although the chief of police paid his respects to his ruler, the act was delivered with reluctance and more than a hint of antagonism.

'Your Highness, I am surprised to see you here at this time of night,' he said, slowly tucking the cap he'd removed from his head under his arm. His black, beady eyes swung to the Sultan's bodyguards protecting them before returning to Zaid.

'Matters of state do not always wait for civilised hours to demand attention.'

The man's gaze settled on her and Esme spied the distinct gleam of malevolence in the black depths. 'And that is what is happening here? A matter of state?'

Zaid's response was spoken in sharp, rapid-fire Arabic, his posture seething with unbridled authority. Esme watch the man shrink back slowly. The hostile expression in his eyes didn't abate, and his gaze darted to her many times during the conversation but he didn't attempt to arrest her.

Although only mere minutes passed, it felt like a lifetime before Zaid glanced her way.

'We're leaving now,' he said.

Relief punched through her and she gave a swift nod as she hurried to match her steps to his.

The moment she slid into the car he climbed in after her. A second later, after she'd slotted in her seat belt, they were moving with the smoothness borne of military precision.

She took a deep, shaky breath, but the thousand questions that crowded Esme's brain were momentarily suppressed when her senses were suffused with the very male scent of the man sitting next to her.

The man staring at her with silent, watchful intensity.

'What…?' She stopped and flicked her tongue over her dry lips. 'Why was he coming to arrest me?'

'Because he found out, like I did, that the allegations you made against his police force weren't entirely accurate. Your interview has been televised every hour for the past twelve hours. There are those who called for your arrest the moment it was aired. It came to my attention that the police chief was beginning to gather his forces.'

Ice cascaded down her spine. 'Oh, my God.' The hand she lifted to push back a swathe of hair shook badly. Tightening it into a fist, she placed it in her lap. 'What…what was he going to charge me with?' Not that it mattered. Jail was jail. And prison in Ja'ahr wasn't something she wanted to experience, even for a minute.

To her surprise, Zaid Al-Ameen's lips pursed before his powerful shoulders moved in a shrug. 'He would've found something.'

'What? You mean he could've just made something up?'

'It could've been something as simple as questioning you about what you said, or it could've been more. You supplied him with all the base he could have wanted. All he needed to do was capitalise on it.'

Her heart dropped to her stomach. 'But isn't that...illegal?' she questioned carefully, unwilling to add further fuel to the fire it seemed she'd started.

In the semi-darkness of the vehicle she watched his jaw clench harshly, his expression turn grave. 'The wheels of change are turning in Ja'ahr, but not fast enough,' he said semi-cryptically. 'True democracy comes at a cost. Not everyone is ready to pay that price yet.'

The bald statement left very little room for more questions after that. The convoy rolled swiftly along near deserted streets, silence reigning in the vehicle. Until Esme realise the familiar road they travelled on.

Her gaze swung from the elevated road and the familiar dome ahead to the man sitting next to her. He was staring at her, shrewd sharp eyes waiting. 'You're taking me—'

'Back to the Royal Palace, yes,' he confirmed.

Wild hysteria powered through her. 'So I was right. You *are* kidnapping me after all.'

She'd meant the words half-jokingly, a way for her tumbling thoughts to grapple with the events of the last hour and the enormity of what might have happened to her.

When he didn't immediately answer, she glanced at him.

The look he levelled at her was in no way mirthful. It

was filled with solemn, unwavering resolve. 'For want of a better word…and for the foreseeable future, yes.'

Zaid watched her process his reply. She may have been joking, but he was deadly serious.

Slowly, every trace of amusement drained from her face. He told himself the apprehension that replaced it was much more useful to him. It would keep her focused properly on what lay ahead of her. It would also serve to draw his attention from the luscious curve of her mouth and the tiny twitch of her nose when she was amused.

He was already battling with the heated tug of his libido at the way her skin had shone under the bathroom lights, like the pearls mined in the sea bordering his kingdom. The way the scrap of silk she had worn to bed had caressed her flesh had made him infinitely glad he'd been wearing a shrouding tunic. The urge to touch her, to relive the memory of holding her warm body captive in his arms was so strong it was a visceral ache deep within him. He smashed down hard on the unwelcome sensation and concentrated on the matter at hand.

'You're serious, aren't you?' Her eyes were widening, her hushed voice stained with burgeoning realisation.

'I have a kingdom to rule. I don't undertake missions like this just for the fun of it.' His words emerged clipped.

She flinched. He experienced the tiniest dart of remorse before he firmed his lips.

Before he could say anything further, his vehicle drew to a stop. His head of security jumped out and opened his door.

Zaid didn't exit immediately. For some reason, he found himself staring at her, taking in her pale features, the lower lip she was worrying as she stared back at him. The shadows under her eyes. 'It's almost two o'clock in the morning.

We will continue this conversation at a more appropriate hour, once you've had some rest.'

He stepped out of the car and held out his hand. Her gaze dropped warily. For a tense moment he watched her silently debate whether or not to take it, then she reached out, almost in slow motion, to finally accept his help.

The sensation of her sliding her hand into his ramped up the volatile tension inside him. Zaid ruthlessly dismissed his body's response, just as he'd dismissed almost all extraneous emotions since his return to Ja'ahr. He'd needed to, to be able to focus on rebuilding what his uncle had so brutally destroyed. It was the reason he hadn't taken a woman to his bed in well over eighteen months. It was the reason his work days were so long and sleep was a luxury he afforded himself only when necessary.

Nevertheless, he found his grip tightening, his touch lingering even after she stood before him, her face upturned to his. In the floodlights gracing the entrance to his palace, her unique beauty struck him all over again.

Enough.

He turned and started to walk away, leaving Fawzi and the rest of his staff to make the arrangements for her care and comfort. Right now there were a hundred other tasks that needed his attention. 'Goodnight, Miss Scott.'

He'd only taken a few steps when heard her rush after him. 'Wait. Please. Your Highness.'

Against his will, Zaid felt the whisper of a smile tug at his lips at the way she'd tagged on his title. Reluctantly. Grudgingly.

Recalling his insistence that she use it the previous afternoon, he grimaced. Although his veins pulsed with royal blood, Zaid had never forced the outer trappings of his nobility on anyone, until her. Something about Esmeralda Scott had made him want to assert his dominion over her. Perhaps, even absurdly, he wanted to see that defiant chin and insubordinate body lowered in the archaic, submissive bow he hated from everyone else.

'Your Highness, please.'

Zaid gritted his teeth and paused at the entrance to the hallway that led to his private lift. The small group of staff who found it necessary to follow him everywhere within the palace, night or day, paused at a respectful distance.

Esmeralda, however, kept coming, her lissom, curvy body swaying sensually beneath the cotton dress. Zaid dragged his gaze from her shapely legs and hips to her face, stamping down once more on the insistent tug to his groin.

'I know it's the middle of the night, but it may as well be the middle of the day for me. I won't be able to sleep. Not until I know more about what's going to…happen.'

To me.

Zaid silently applauded her for leaving those words out. She was determined to show no weakness, despite the precarious position in which she'd placed herself and her father. A situation he'd been monitoring since she'd left his office the previous afternoon. The repercussions of her interview had been more damaging than he'd initially thought. He'd been in the process of considering ways to mitigate it when he'd been alerted to the chief of police's intentions.

Recollection of their conversation in the hotel foyer made him grit his teeth. If Esmeralda Scott wanted to know what fruit her actions had borne, he would gladly apprise her. And since he hadn't been heading for his own bed, now was as good a time as any.

He dismissed his staff, although he knew Fawzi and his bodyguards would remain awake and in close proximity until Zaid himself retired to bed. 'Very well. We will talk now,' he said to her.

He caught her quick, nervous swallow before she gave a firm, responding nod. 'Lead the way, Your Highness.'

Zaid didn't know whether to commend her fearlessness or condemn her for it, because the spirit she'd displayed, which had led her into hot water in the first place, would be what she would need to keep her going in the days to come. He was still tossing the thought around in his head when he entered his private lift. She followed him into the small space, but immediately plastered herself to the wall farthest from him. Zaid would have been amused by the action if his senses hadn't been immediately assailed with the delicate scent of her cherry blossom shampoo and the elusive wisps of perfume that clung to her skin.

The moment the doors shut, her breathing altered. Her eyes darted to him and he noted that they reflected more green than grey with her suppressed agitation. When he leaned forward to press the button, she jumped and he smiled.

'I'm glad you find this amusing, Your Highness.'

'I will take my amusements where I please since I interrupted my night to come to your aid. A task for which you have yet to thank me.'

She hesitated for a moment before she answered. 'You told me less than five minutes ago that you've effectively kidnapped me. Pardon me for not reserving the right to find out first if I've been whisked from one undesirable situation into another before frothing at the mouth with gratitude.'

With a magnetic pull he couldn't resist, his gaze dropped to her mouth again. Rouged from the distressed biting of moments ago, the plump Cupid's bow was more enticing than he wanted to acknowledge. Again it took an irritatingly large amount of control to drag his gaze away.

'I look forward to witnessing this...frothing when the time comes.'

He exited the lift straight into the office he preferred to use when he wasn't attending to scheduled matters of state.

Zaid crossed to the extensive drinks cabinet and looked over his shoulder. 'Would you like something to drink?'

'No, thank you,' she murmured, a touch distractedly.

Her gaze was taking in the less formal layout of the room—the grouping of large cushions centred around a Bedouin carpet said to have been woven by his great-grandmother, with the rarely used hookah set on a bronze tray in the middle of it; the half-divan tucked beneath an arched window, upon which lay a set of papers and his reading glasses. The suit jacket hanging at the back of a chair, and the *keffiyeh* he'd discarded hours ago when he'd come upstairs.

Zaid wasn't sure why seeing her gaze on his personal effects strummed the pulsing hunger within him. But as he turned to pour a glass of mineral water, he considered that perhaps the time had come to attend to his baser needs. Before it impinged on clear and concise thinking. Just as quickly as the thought had come, he was already discarding it. He had neither the time nor inclination to pursue any of the women from his past life, nor did he feel compelled to entertain the advances of noble families both in Ja'ahr and its prosperous neighbours, wishing to marry off their daughters to the new Sultan.

The time was coming when he'd have to do his duty, marry and produce heirs. He knew that. But not before he'd attempted to bring change to Ja'ahr and set it on a much more stable course. He didn't just owe it to his people, he owed it to the memory of his parents, who'd been assassinated in the name of power and greed.

The raw reminder helped him suppress the primal hunger caused by the presence of the woman now turning to face him again.

'You have questions,' he stated, after finishing his drink

and setting down his glass. 'If you're going to demand to leave come morning, let me pre-empt that by saying I don't foresee this being a situation that will be resolved in twenty-four hours so, no, you won't be leaving any time soon.'

Her lips parted, but she didn't immediately reply. She took a moment to absorb his words before she spoke again. 'I understand now that things are done a little...differently here. But I need to know what *any time soon* entails. I can't stay here indefinitely. I have a life to get back to.'

'Eventually, but not immediately,' he said.

She frowned. 'What?'

'You flew to Ja'ahr to support your father, did you not? I believe you've taken a month's leave of absence from work for that purpose.'

Her eyes widened. 'How do you know that?'

'I make it my business to know pertinent details surrounding my cases. Of course, your conduct yesterday afternoon also warranted a little more research into you personally.'

Zaid couldn't recall moving closer to her but suddenly they were mere feet apart. He knew it because he could see the green-grey shades of her eyes much more clearly, read the bewilderment in her expression and the rapid pulse beating at her throat.

He shoved his hands into his trouser pockets to kill the urge to splay his fingers over that silken pulse.

'Surely you can't expect me to remain here for all that time? Besides, you spoke to the chief of police, didn't you? That's why he didn't arrest me tonight?' she pressed.

Zaid shrugged. 'I bought you a temporary reprieve, but let me lay it out for you so there's no mistake. Attempt to leave this palace before I deem it safe for you to do so, and you will be arrested and imprisoned. The chief has some influence in the right circles.'

Esmeralda shook her head, her puzzlement evident as her gaze probed his. The action caused the long sheaf of her ponytail to swing, drawing his gaze to the thick rope of hair. Zaid didn't welcome the reminder of the way it had looked unbound. After a moment, she turned away, hugging her arms to her middle as she paced to the edge of the floor cushions. In the silence that pulsed between them his gaze dropped, tracing over her slim shoulders to her delicate spine and the womanly flaring of hips and curve of buttocks to the shapely length of her legs.

The sudden image of her lying on top of his cushions, wearing nothing but that saucy little see-through night slip, with her hair spread out over his pillows, punched so hard through him that his stomach muscles clenched viciously.

The fists in his pockets bunched tighter, and he veiled his eyes as she whirled back around.

'I still don't understand. Why did you save...um, come to my aid at all?'

It took precious seconds for his mind to track long enough to refocus on the decision he'd made the previous afternoon.

Raising his gaze, he reaffirmed the fact that Esmeralda Scott would not be gracing his cushions or anywhere else in his personal space. Not unless he wanted to court trouble. The woman in front of him had been in his kingdom for only a short time, and yet she'd already caused ripples that could destabilise everything he'd worked so hard for. It was time to draw some boundaries and put her firmly in her place.

'No matter your failings, I've decided you're more useful to me out of prison than in it.'

CHAPTER FIVE

'USEFUL?' ESME ECHOED.

Dark eyes gleamed at her, the haughty expression having deepened between the time she'd paced to and from the stunning arrangement of cushions on the floor. But alongside that expression she sensed something else, something that accelerated her heartbeat. Something she desperately wanted to deny. But no matter how hard she tried, a part of her brain remained locked on the magnificence of the man before her.

In her hotel room, fear and adrenaline had ruled, dictating her actions, although the keen awareness of him had been present too. Now, in the soft, exotic luxury of the lamplit room filled with his towering presence, her awareness of him had heightened to far more disturbing proportions.

'Do you need the word defined for you? I have a need for you other than as an inmate wasting away in my prison cell.'

She shook her head in confusion, an action she seemed to have repeated a few times in his presence. 'Let me get this straight. You didn't come to my aid out of the goodness of your heart but rather on the basis of what I could give you?'

The moment she said the words she realised how needy and damning they sounded. But the all-powerful man in front of her didn't give an indication that he cared one way or the other.

Zaid Al-Ameen merely shrugged, his hands easing out of his pockets to remove the robe that layered his tunic and drape it lazily over an armchair. 'Primarily. But there's room to negotiate what you could stand to gain from this arrangement.'

Through the prickling of an even sharper awareness at the sight of the impressive chest and muscles straining beneath the black tunic, Esme absorbed his words.

He wanted something from her.

Just like her father did and had done for the endless years before she'd been forced to walk away from him. Just like everyone did at one point or another in her interaction with them.

The emotion that lodged in her chest felt absurdly like hurt. Absurd because in no way should this man have the power to wound her. She'd barely known him for a day.

Pushing the feeling away, she tightened the arms clasped around her middle and returned his stare. 'And what arrangement would that be, exactly? Your Highness?' She tagged on the title to remind herself of the vast differences between them.

'Reparations for the damage you've caused,' he stated imperiously.

'Reparations?' Damn it, she really needed to stop parroting his words. 'But I have nothing to give you.'

'On the contrary, I have a need for you that would restore some goodwill in your favour.'

Her spine tingled with premonition. 'I'm sorry, you've lost me.'

His long arms clasped behind his back, the movement tugging her attention once again to the ripple of muscle beneath cotton. 'You're a social worker, are you not?'

She frowned. 'Yes.'

'There are organisations here in Ja'ahr that could use your expertise. While you're here, you will work for me.'

'Work for you? Doing what?'

'Exactly what you do back in England, helping displaced families and offering practical guidance to young adults who need it.'

She reeled at his accurate description of her role at Touch Global. 'Just how much research did you do on me?' she asked, a thudding starting in her chest at the prospect of Zaid Al-Ameen finding out everything about her, including the one incident she could never wash from her soul.

'I know relevant details.'

The imprecise response didn't bring a single ounce of relief. But she clung to the hope that if he'd gone searching for facts about her work, then Sultan Zaid wouldn't have uncovered her most damning secret.

But the man you're dealing with is a ruthless prosecutor also known as The Butcher.

Her relief collapsed under the stark reminder.

'Do I have your agreement?' Zaid pressed.

She yanked herself from the black abyss of her past and shook her head. 'No. I'm not...' She stumbled to a halt, her mind reeling at what he'd demanded of her.

'It was your wish to speak now, instead of in the morning when you would have had some sleep. It's not too late to take that option if it'll help you be less confused.'

His faint mocking tone sparked heat in her cheeks. 'I'm not confused, just...' She stopped again and took a breath. 'Well, for starters, I have no clue how your social care system works.'

He paced closer. She had to tilt her head to meet his gaze. The sensation of being small in his presence registered once again. 'The basics of social care are the same no matter where you are in the world,' he said.

She couldn't disagree. 'Okay, but there are other things to consider.'

'Such as?'

'The language barrier, for one thing.'

'Children are taught English alongside their Arabic lessons. Every citizen in Ja'ahr speaks English. Communication won't be a problem.'

Esme couldn't deny that everywhere she'd been since her arrival, she'd been met with impeccably spoken English. 'I'm only here for a month. To support my father. Everything else would be secondary to that. What good would that do anyone? And even if that weren't an issue, where would I live?'

'Here in the palace,' he responded in a low, deep voice.

'With you?'

An inscrutable look fleeted across his face, gone too quickly for her to catch, but it didn't stop another tingle of awareness from stinging her skin.

'Under my roof,' he clarified. 'Under my protection.'

The tiny catch of her breath somewhere in her midriff told her she was affording far too much importance to his words. Dozens of people lived in the Royal Palace. She would be one of many. Nothing special.

'As to how long you intend to be here,' he continued, 'if you'd taken time to do a little more research, you would've found out that a month wouldn't be anywhere near an accurate timescale to give yourself.'

'That was all I was entitled to.'

'Then an extension will need to be obtained from your employer if you truly intend to be here for your father for the entirety of the legal proceedings. I can request it from Touch Global on your behalf, if you wish. Or you can see to it yourself. Either way, the only thing that'll happen in the next four weeks is the setting of your father's trial date hearing.'

She should have waited till morning to discuss this but, then, how much deeper would he have probed and strategised?

Esme frowned. 'It takes a whole month to obtain a trial date? I thought you were pushing for an expedited trial?'

'Yes, and that won't be for six months at the earliest.'

Shock punched the breath from her lungs. *'Six months?'*

'Yes. Were I to request a normal trial, he would be looking at two years in jail before his case was even heard.'

Her eyes widened. 'You have that many untried people languishing in your prisons?' She cringed the moment the guileless words left her lips.

His head jerked back anyway, his eyes growing a touch colder. 'I believe I've already mentioned the ways in which change comes. The pursuit of zero tolerance accountability also has its unique challenges.'

Esme bit her lip, and judged it wise to choose her battles. 'I'm...sorry, I didn't mean to criticise the way you run your country. Your Highness.'

She caught another gleam in his eyes at her use of his title a second before his lashes swept low and concealed his expression, but his answer to her response was to stroll past her to the conference table. As she watched, he pressed a button on a futuristic-looking gadget sitting on the polished surface and issued fast, lyrical Arabic before he turned back to her.

'My staff will escort you to your suite. We will speak again in the morning when you are better rested.' The dismissal was final.

'But I need—'

He gave a single, implacable shake of his head, his jet-black hair gleaming beneath the soft lit chandelier. 'I have other matters to attend to, Miss Scott.'

A glance at the grand antique clock proudly displayed on his wall showed it was almost three a.m. 'At this time of night?'

'The office of the King never sleeps.'

'What about the King himself? Does he sleep? Or is he

superhuman?' she asked, before she thought better of it. To be fair, she told herself, he *looked* superhuman enough to attest to the fact that sleep was a very minor impediment that could be overlooked at will.

A knock came on the door a moment later but, unlike before, no one entered. It became clear that whoever he'd summoned was waiting for his permission to enter. Permission he withheld as he stared at her for a long, charged moment.

'You wish to discuss my sleep patterns, Miss Scott?' The question was softly voiced, but the low rumble of his tone pulsed with a new, sensual danger that heated the blood in her veins.

Despite the shifting sands beneath her feet, Esme didn't heed the warning. Esmeralda, she wanted to say. *Call me Esmeralda.* She bit off the urge at the last moment, blindly stabbing at another, more grounding question. 'I wanted to discuss what you would do if I refused you come morning. If I say no, what then?'

Everything hardened. His eyes. His face. His body. In that moment, she became fully intimate with the reason he'd earned his moniker.

'I would advise you against it because if you refuse, we will be having a very different conversation,' he rasped.

She was gritting her teeth against the chill his words brought when the door opened and Fawzi entered. Despite the late hour, he was sharp-eyed and alert, his posture ramrod straight after bowing to his master. Without taking his eyes off her, Zaid spoke in low, firm tones to his private secretary, who nodded.

'If you would come with me, Madam, your staff is waiting to escort you to your suite.'

Surprise helped her break the power of Zaid's stare. 'My *staff*?'

Fawzi tensed, once again perturbed at her direct address to him in his Sultan's presence.

'Each guest in the Royal Palace is assigned their own staff for the duration of their stay,' Zaid supplied silkily. The timbre of his tone dared her to take umbrage with that.

Esme chose retreat instead, even though something inside her pinched in disappointment that their conversation was over. 'Goodnight, Your Highness.'

As she turned to leave, she caught the mocking tilt of Zaid's brow. She silently cursed the wave of heat that rose again, studiously keeping her face averted as she followed his private secretary to the door. The ripple of awareness down her spine told her Zaid's sharp gaze stayed with her until she was out of view.

At which point, she once again experienced a plummeting of her mood. All that disappeared the moment she was faced with two women wearing varying expressions of curiosity. The older woman, dressed in a deep purple *abaya* and headscarf, was more successful at keeping her expression neutral than the younger woman, who stared at Esme with open interest.

'This is Nashwa and her assistant, Aisha.' Fawzi introduced them. 'Nashwa is in charge of the guest suites in the south wing. I will leave you in their care.'

He hurried away, leaving an awkward little silence in his wake before Esme recalled that these two women most likely spoke English.

She attempted a small smile. 'I apologise if you were woken up because of me.'

'We are here to serve at His Highness's pleasure,' Nashwa replied, gesturing gracefully to one of the many well-lit corridors that led away from Zaid's office. 'No command will ever be too great.'

Aisha nodded enthusiastically, smiling as she cast a furtive glance at Esme.

'Well, thank you, all the same,' Esme said.

Nashwa nodded, the soft fall of her gown brushing the floor as she led the way at a brisk pace.

Esme couldn't help her gasp at first sight of the elegant salmon-pink and rose-gold room she'd been allocated.

The highly polished marble floor flowed from the doorway and into the large living room. Just before the gorgeously upholstered set of sofas arranged on a Persian rug, the largest bouquet of flowers she'd ever seen had been arranged in a giant vase atop a round console table made of black lacquered wood inlaid with mother-of-pearl.

'The bedroom is this way, Madam,' Nashwa urged in a soft voice.

Esme dragged her gaze from the white baby grand piano that adorned the room and followed through a smaller set of doors.

She barely managed to suppress another gasp as she was confronted with a king-sized bed whose carved posts were painted in swirling designs of pure rose gold. Muslin curtains fluttered in cascading drapes around the pristinely covered bed, while on either side, large Moroccan lamps glowed on twin bedside tables. Smaller bouquets holding long-stemmed exotic orchids sat on the tables and when she took a breath, Esme inhaled their delicate scent.

'We took the liberty of unpacking for you, Madam. Aisha will help you with your night things or, if you prefer, we have provided you with alternative clothing.'

Following Nashwa's direction, Esme spotted a set of lingerie folded neatly on the bed. She wasn't aware she'd moved over the plush carpet until her fingers caressed the silk and lace concoction. The slip was short and similarly styled to the one she owned but with a matching robe and made of far more expensive material than her own.

Beautiful, expensive things. All around her. Things meant to be admired. Decadently enjoyed. Except everything came at a price. She'd known it from the moment her father had given her an unimaginable choice on her fourteenth birthday—foster care or boarding school with her holidays spent on the road with him. With her mother's abandonment a fresh trauma in her reality, choosing her father for a few months of the year, despite the knowledge that he was prepared to abandon her too, had felt like her only option. Until that life too had come crashing down on her head.

'Would Madam prefer this set?' Nashwa enquired.

Esme snatched her hand away, the memories and the notion that things were spinning out of her control churning faster until she felt nauseous.

'No, thank you.' She stopped, cleared her husky throat and summoned a smile. 'If you don't mind showing me where my things are?'

The older woman nodded immediately, her diplomacy firmly back in place. 'Of course, Madam.' She led the way to a dressing room and adjoining bathroom that was bigger than Esme's flat back in London.

Amongst the vast square footage of empty shelves and drawers, her meagre belongings looked forlorn occupying a single shelf. The absence of her peach night slip reminded her she was still wearing it under her dress. Unbidden, her mind skipped back to the hotel room and the sizzling effect of Zaid's gaze on her just a few short hours ago. Heat threatened to fire up again as her body tightened in recollection.

'Do you need assistance in undressing?'

Esme jumped guiltily at the softly voiced question and turned to see Aisha gliding forward with a smile.

She shook her head, then raised her hand to rub the tension headache that was making its presence felt at her temples.

'Some chamomile tea perhaps, to aid a restful sleep?' Nashwa urged.

Esme dropped her hand as weariness seeped into her bones. 'Normally I would say yes, but I don't think I'll need it. I'm ready to drop off.'

Aisha took that as a sign to make herself busy else-where, and Esme emerged from a quick trip to the bath-room to find that she had indeed been busy. The covers of the bed were turned down, a crystal jug of water and a glass stood on her bedside table, and the lamps were dimmed to a pleasant glow.

Both women were standing just inside the bedroom doors. With twin curtsies, they bade her goodnight and left.

Alone at last, she slipped off her dress and slid between the sheets, replaying the day's mind-boggling cascade of events. Esme wasn't unfamiliar with how one decision could change the course of one's life. She'd lived through one such unforgettable event at seventeen, and wore the scars to prove it. But even she couldn't have foreseen how a three-minute interview could have set off such a roller-coaster.

A roller-coaster that had only slowed momentarily. Come daylight, she would once again be fighting to hold on, because Zaid Al-Ameen wasn't done with her. She in-tended to push for a visit to her father but whether or not that plea would be granted was another matter.

It was still uppermost in her mind the moment she opened her eyes. Contrary to thinking she would toss and turn for the rest of the night, she'd slept soundly, waking to the sound of a bath being run and the scent of eucalyptus and crushed roses in the air.

Nashwa's courteous greeting and apology for waking her was followed by the announcement that the Sultan wished to see her within the hour.

After bathing, she secured her hair in a neat bun, slipped into her short-sleeved chocolate shirtdress and cinched the wide gold belt in place. The three-inch leather wedges and a touch of light make-up finished the ensemble, and five minutes later, after navigating a dozen or so corridors, she was shown into a large dining room.

Zaid was already seated at the head of the table, with two butlers standing to attention next to a sideboard heaving with food. The room, like every one she'd seen so far, was stunning beyond words, every inch draped in breathtaking masterpieces.

She would never get used to the jaw-dropping beauty of Ja'ahr's Royal Palace, but her senses were over-saturated with it. So it was easy to focus on the man dressed in a different set of traditional clothes, this time a dark gold with black trim. Or so she told herself. Deep down, she was unwilling to admit that his presence in any room in the world would command immediate and complete attention.

The black *keffiyeh* secured with gold ropes framing his head threw his sharp, handsome features into stunning relief. But the eyes that swept over her body to meet her eyes were the cause of the dipping and diving in her belly as she made her way down the long banquet table towards him.

Just like the first time they'd met, he rose to his feet, the gallant greeting belying the primitive aura that surrounded his hard, lean body. She didn't want to admit that she found it sexy. Just as she didn't want to admit that the whole package that comprised Sultan Zaid Al-Ameen was so alluring it threatened to trigger another tongue-tied episode. Fear of that happening caused Esme to force out the words tripping on her tongue.

'I want to see my father. Before any further discussion happens between us, I want to see him,' she said the moment she reached him.

'Good morning, Esmeralda. I trust you slept well?' he drawled after a telling bubble of silence.

Embarrassment temporarily swamped every other emotion. She inwardly grimaced at her lack of grace. 'I'm sorry. Good morning, Your Highness.'

He stepped towards her and pulled out her chair. About to sink gratefully into it, she froze when she felt him lean towards her. 'Despite your questionable manners, since there is a great chance we'll be in each other's company for a while, you may drop the formalities when we are alone.'

Her head swivelled to his in surprise, and then other *urgent* sensations took over when she realised how close he was. Heat from his body buffeted hers, along with the lingering scent of soap and aftershave that punched a potent awareness straight into her bloodstream.

'I… What should I call you, then?' she murmured.

His gaze drifted over her face, lingering on her lips before rising to meet hers once more. 'My given name will suffice,' he replied.

Her mouth tingling, she attempted to nod. When she barely succeeded in moving her head, she swallowed and tried her voice instead. 'I… Okay.'

That damnable brow lifted. 'Okay? Perhaps you should try using my name. Let's be sure it is satisfactory to both of us. Perhaps in a morning greeting?'

'Good morning… Zaid.'

Brandy-coloured eyes turned a shade darker. He stared at her for a handful of seconds before his lids swept down, masking his gaze. This close, Esme couldn't help but appreciate the indecently long male beauty of his lashes. Too soon, he speared her with those piercing eyes, his mouth quirking when he caught her staring.

'Sit down, Esmeralda. Our breakfast is getting cold.'

She sat. She even managed to chew and swallow a few morsels of food. All in silence while several members of staff approached to speak to Zaid. Belatedly, she realised that for him this was a working breakfast. She was thankful for the chance to collect her scattered thoughts.

What she wasn't thankful for was the ominous approach of Fawzi as they were finishing their meal. The sixth sense she'd honed during her time with her father warned her that whatever news he was about to deliver wouldn't be welcome.

To give him his due, he didn't glance her way once. But even before he bent to murmur in his master's ear, even before Zaid's jaw clenched and he cast a glance at her, Esme's belly was rolling with dread.

'What is it? What's happened?' she demanded the moment Fawzi straightened.

'It looks like you'll get to see your father much sooner than planned. There's been another altercation at the prison.'

CHAPTER SIX

ESME HURRIED TO keep up with Zaid's strides, although she had no idea where they were headed. He'd merely risen from his chair and instructed her to come with him.

'How could there have been another altercation? He's still in the prison hospital,' she said.

'No, he's not. Apparently, he was moved back to his cell in the middle of the night.'

Her heart lurched. 'And he's been attacked again already?'

'The details are still sketchy. But I'll have answers within the hour.'

She believed him. The grim set of his jaw and the purpose to his stride told her so. What she didn't realise until they approached double doors manned by sentries who swung them open to reveal a walled terrace was that he intended on seeking the answers first-hand.

Stone steps led down to meticulously landscaped gardens that rolled for almost a quarter mile. In the middle of it all, on a patch of grass, a helipad the size of two tennis courts held three helicopters with the royal insignia emblazoned on their gleaming frames.

Time slowed, along with her feet. A loud buzzing sounded in her ears, her palms growing clammy as she stared at the helicopter that Zaid was heading towards. Dry-mouthed, she urged her feet to move, but it was like being stuck in treacle.

Zaid, noticing that she wasn't beside him, turned sharply. Esme sensed more than saw his frown. 'Is something the matter?' he demanded.

The sound of his voice brought time rushing back,

fast-forwarded in a kaleidoscope of shameful, cutting memories.

Vegas.

A thrilling helicopter ride over the Grand Canyon.

Hopeful smiles and a stumbling proposal of marriage. Bryan's haunting expression when he'd discovered the truth—

'What is wrong? Are you feeling unwell?' came the sharp query.

Esme jumped, blinking back into the present and the man whose towering shadow dwarfed her.

He was staring at her with a puzzled frown, one that grew darker with each second.

'I… I'm not a fan of helicopters.'

His eyes narrowed. 'You suffer from vertigo?'

It would have been so easy to lie and say yes. But the opposite was true. Her first and last ride on a helicopter had been an exhilarating experience. It was what had come after that shot raw pain through her. Her father had laid the trap, but she'd unwittingly led Bryan into it. For that she would never forgive herself. She'd known what her father was like. 'Not exactly.'

'Then what *exactly*?'

'I just don't like them.'

'Not even when they're the quickest means of getting you to your father?' His tone suggested he found her reluctance odd.

'How long will a car journey take?'

'Too long, considering the inmates are on the verge of a full-blown riot.'

Her breath caught. 'What?'

'Your father isn't the only person I'm concerned about, Esmeralda. So if you wish to get to him quickly, we need to go.'

She swallowed, glanced at the aircraft and nodded. 'Okay, I'll come.'

As if he didn't totally believe her, he grasped her elbow. Her already frenzied senses spun even faster, a shiver coursing down her spine as they neared the helicopter.

If Zaid noticed, he didn't react. His attention was focused on the sharply dressed pilot who gave a stiff salute and held the door open. One bodyguard climbed in beside the pilot and another four scrambled into the second aircraft.

Zaid helped her up and she slid to the far side of the chopper. The two bench seats facing one another were cut off from the pilot section, affording them complete privacy. And unlike her first ride, Esme noted the moment the door shut that they wouldn't need headphones in order to communicate. The space was completely soundproof.

A fact confirmed when Zaid settled into the seat opposite her and instructed in a low, deep voice, 'Put on your seat belt.'

She fumbled to comply, very much aware the eyes that rested on her remained inquisitive.

She glanced over at him, to find his unwavering gaze still pinned on her. 'I'm fine now. You don't need to be concerned that I'll freak out again.'

'Do you want to explain why you chose such a critical time to go into a trance?' he asked.

She bit her inner lip. One of the many vows she'd made to herself when she'd walked away from her father eight years ago had been never to engage in the subterfuge Jeffrey Scott loved to indulge in. The truth, no matter how brutal, was always preferable to lies. If she'd confronted the truth eight years ago, seen her father for who he really was, Bryan might still be alive.

But telling Zaid the unvarnished truth right now would be opening not just herself but also her father up to total annihilation because Zaid was still the prosecutor intent on putting her father away. She could, however, offer an explanation without incriminating herself or her father.

'I had a bad experience after a helicopter ride a long time ago.'

'Where?' he fired back.

'Does it matter?'

He didn't answer. At least not with his lips anyway. His eyebrow, however, lifted in direct challenge of her defensive response.

She glanced out of the window, noted the severely dilapidated landscape abutting the desert in the distance. 'In... Las Vegas.'

'You were with a lover?' he asked.

Her gaze flew to his, her breath crushing in her lungs at the bold demand stamped across his face.

She wanted to tell him that it was none of his business.

But somehow, in that moment, denying Bryan's existence felt like dishonouring the man who'd been marked just by associating with her.

She prevaricated for a moment, then exhaled. 'I was with someone who cared about me.' Bryan hadn't been her lover. But he was the reason she'd never taken a lover. He was the reason that, at twenty-five, she was still a virgin.

'You were the reason the experience ended badly?'

His mildly condemning tone made her insides clench. 'Why would you assume that?'

'I wouldn't be good at my profession if simple deduction eluded me that easily, Esmeralda. Besides, a high percentage of couples who take such helicopter rides are already involved or about to be. You choose your words carefully, but correct me if I'm mistaken that things ended badly because you had a change of heart about advancing the relationship?'

He struck so close to the truth it robbed her of breath.

He took her slack-jawed look as confirmation, and his gaze hardened. 'Let me guess, he wanted to take things to the next level, and you suddenly decided you had somewhere else to be?'

'You make me sound so…calculating.' Which was such an apt description of Jeffrey Scott's annihilation of Bryan, she suppressed a shiver.

'Do I? If not that, then what? What was this bad experience that still makes you green at the gills with guilt?' His voice was harsher, his expression haughtily superior.

He'd seen her guilt. She had nowhere to hide. 'He… proposed to me…after the helicopter ride.'

Sharp, narrowed eyes darted to her bare left hand, then back to her face. 'And you said no, obviously.' Why was there such a thick vein of satisfaction in his voice? Was he that glad that he'd proved her as callous as she'd been forced to be with Bryan?

'Yes, I said no. I couldn't marry him.' For one thing, she'd been not quite eighteen to Bryan's twenty-one. For another, she hadn't been in love with him. And that was even before she'd discovered what her father had done to him.

'Why not?'

'I just couldn't.'

Although his gaze remained on her, he didn't probe further. Which was a relief, since everything that had occurred afterwards ate like acid in her belly, even after all this time. The pain of it would never go away. Someday it might lessen, enough for her to forge something of a life she could be proud of. Until then, her work would be her life.

The sudden dip of the helicopter had her gripping her seat, her heart tripping over itself. A quick look out the window showed they were approaching their destination. Like most prisons in the world, this one too consisted of large, interconnecting buildings ring-fenced by miles of menacing barbed wire, towers with guards armed to the teeth. Despite the awful things he'd done, the thought of her father spending the rest of his days there—

'Easy,' Zaid drawled from across her. 'You're in danger of ripping the seat to shreds.'

Esme looked down. Her knuckles were white from her death grip on the soft leather. With a deep breath, she released her hold on it, but her gaze returned to the looming structure. There were no outward signs of unrest. Which should have brought a little relief. Until her gaze flickered once more to Zaid.

'Should you be here?'

Dark brows clamped in a frown. 'Excuse me?'

'You're the Sultan. You're also the man who presumably put a lot of the criminals in there behind bars. Aren't you...won't you be exposing yourself to...um, danger at the prison?'

His brow slowly cleared. 'Are you concerned about my welfare, Esmeralda?' The softly voiced question rumbled between them, gaining an electric note that sent a jolt of awareness through her.

'I'm merely making a pertinent observation,' she replied.

The dangerous sensuality left his expression, replaced by the merciless resolution she was beginning to associate with the ruler of Ja'ahr. 'You expect me to cower behind the safety of my palace walls in times of crisis?'

It was the last thing she expected. His presence in her hotel room alone when he needn't have come to her aid at all was testament to the fact that Zaid Al-Ameen didn't back down from confrontations.

Letting his police chief take her would have been one less problem for him to contend with. Instead, he'd done the opposite. 'No, but that doesn't mean you should rush into danger either. What if…something happens to you?'

'So you *are* troubled by the idea of harm coming to me.' His voice held definite mockery, but it also held another ephemeral note. One that stroked her senses, and drew her gaze magnetically to his. The gold flecks that swirled through his eyes were almost hypnotic, transmitting a call that struck a curious hunger within her. When his gaze dropped to her lips, Esme's breath stuttered then died in her lungs. The need to slick her tongue over the tingling lower lip grew too strong to resist. She watched his eyes darken as he followed the slow glide.

'Being concerned about someone's safety is an act of common decency. Is that so bad?' Her voice was a husky murmur laden with emotions she didn't want to name.

A touch of hard cynicism fleeted over his face. 'In my experience, most acts of selflessness come at a price. I have learned that it's better to look a gift horse in the mouth. That way you know exactly what you're getting.'

The helicopter jostled gently as it rotated and landed with barely a bump on a designated platform near the outer perimeter of the prison. Zaid made no move to get out. Neither did she. The cocoon they were wrapped in felt too intimate, too powerful to break.

'You're entitled to your opinion, I suppose. But I assure you, my concern doesn't come with a price.'

'Perhaps not in this instance. Can you say the same for the future?' he queried.

'I can't predict the future, Zaid. Neither can you.'

His smile didn't touch his eyes, and his gaze flicked from her eyes to her mouth and back again, as if he couldn't look away. 'But it's in my interest to mitigate against it.'

'And that includes any emotional support offered to you? What kind of life is that?'

'One that grants me a high percentage of not being

surprised by the unexpected. I much prefer to see things coming than not.'

She shook her head, unable to come up with an appropriate response. Another handful of seconds passed, then he lifted his hand in a subtle, graceful command.

The doors slid back. Just like in the early hours of this morning, he alighted first, then turned to take her hand.

She attempted to guard herself against the pulse of erotic static she suspected would strike again when she touched him. But it was no use. The moment her palm brushed his, tiny volts of electricity shot over her skin. The short, sharp breath she sucked in was echoed by a more masculine sound from him.

Esme wasn't sure whether to be pleased or terrified that Zaid was just as affected as she was. Since Bryan she'd taken pains to avoid any form of emotional entanglement. The cost of her single mistake had been too much to ever risk letting her guard down. Nevertheless, the notion that she wasn't in this alone, that she wasn't imagining this powerful chemistry between them, was slightly easier to bear. Besides, from what he'd said only minutes ago, Zaid had no intention of letting any of this...disquieting reaction affect him. So her panic was unnecessary.

Satisfied with that conclusion, she stepped out beside him, even risked a glance at the dominant, patrician features of the King. To find his own gaze fixed on her with an intensity that made the hairs rise on her nape.

'Had we the time, I would be curious to know what machinations were being hatched behind that exquisite face,' he murmured.

Any response from her was forestalled by the swift arrival of a tall, lean man. He barely spared her a glance, his brisk bow and effusive greeting reserved for his Sultan.

But after a minute Zaid turned to her, no trace of the jittery sensation that still fizzed beneath her skin visible on his face. He was back to being the imperial overlord of his desert kingdom. 'This is the warden of the prison. He has arranged for you to see your father, while I attend to other matters.'

They sailed through three security checkpoints and arrived at a surprisingly well-appointed reception hall.

'Your father will be brought to you presently, Miss Scott,' the warden stiffly informed her, gesturing to one of the seats.

'Thank you,' she replied, then, as if drawn by a magnet, her gaze darted back to Zaid. He was clearly issuing instructions in Arabic to two of his bodyguards. She watched, stunned, as they approached and flanked her. Zaid's eyes met hers for an instant, then he turned and left the room with the warden.

The notion that she was under guard should have disturbed her. Except, again, the notion that Zaid was ensuring her safety assumed paramount proportions in her mind.

Or he's making sure you won't attempt to do anything else to embarrass him.

She was mulling that over when the doors opened.

Esme's heart jumped into her throat.

Despite the wheelchair he sat in, he was still restrained, the chains binding his hands connected to his ankles over the cuffs of his dark grey jumpsuit. But that wasn't the most shocking aspect of the prisoner rolling forward towards her.

The Jeffrey Scott she'd walked away from eight years ago had been the quintessential English gentleman, impeccable from the carefully groomed hair, slightly greying the temples, right down to the Oxford wingtip shoes he'd favoured.

The man in front of her was painfully thin, with severely dishevelled, shocking white hair and a full, unkempt beard. His skin was sallow, his cheeks and forehead grazed with signs of the fight he'd been involved in.

He saw her shock and gave a wry smile as the grim-faced guard applied the brakes to the wheelchair and retreated to a watchful distance.

They stared at each other for a long minute before he indicated his chains and gave a bitter laugh. 'I know I look a dreadful sight. Not like you, though.'

And just like that the faint tendrils of guilt that had always dwelled beneath the surface of her relationship with her father threatened to resurface.

Before Esme had come along, her parents had lived a high-octane lifestyle financed through fraud. Then Abigail Scott had got pregnant and decided to settle down. Her father had managed enforced domesticity for a few years, but had eventually succumbed to his old ways. Their disagreements and unhappiness had finally culminated in her mother walking out when Esme was fourteen. Abigail had moved to the Australian outback and was killed in a horse-riding accident barely a year later.

For months after her mother had left, she'd watched her father grapple with what to do with her. The ultimatum of boarding school with holidays spent with him or foster care had been delivered with the clear expectation that she would choose the latter option. He was all she had left in the world, for better or worse. It was why Esme had chosen to spend her holidays with him, even though she'd disapproved of his lifestyle. Better that than foster care.

It wasn't until it was too late that she'd realised just how unlovable she was to the man who should have loved and cared for her during her childhood. Perhaps being cast adrift in the foster care system would have been preferable.

She pushed the pain back now and returned her father's gaze as he continued, 'You look very well, Esmeralda. Even better than you did on TV.'

'You saw the broadcast?'

He smiled, eyes the same shade as hers twinkling wickedly. 'Only about a dozen times, until the warden banned it. Thanks for giving them hell.'

Esme winced. 'I may have caused more harm than good.'

He shrugged. 'Who cares?'

She frowned. 'I do.'

His smile dimmed, a harsher look entering his eyes. 'You have a soft heart. That's always been your downfall. But don't beat yourself up about it. You achieved what you wanted, didn't you?'

'At what price, though? Isn't there a riot brewing now because of it?'

His chains rattled as he waved away her concern. 'A riot is always brewing in this place.' After a quick glance at the guard, he leaned forward and said under his breath, 'But we can work all this to our advantage. The moment I saw you on TV, I knew things were looking up.'

'You couldn't possibly have predicted this?'

He sent her a droll look. 'How many times did you see me place the most unlikely bet and come out on top?'

Her unease grew, her heart picking up its beat as she stared at him. 'So you gambled with your health, with your *life*?'

He sat back with a huff. 'What life? I'd much rather throw a final dice than end up here for the long term. And I was right to do so, wasn't I? The rumours are true? You're living with Sultan Al-Ameen at the Royal Palace?'

'How do you—?' She stopped and shook her head. 'No, not in that way—'

'Don't lie to me!'

A knot of anger burst through her. 'I'm not lying! And I don't intend to, not for you, or for anyone.'

'That's a shame. You could have been so good at it if you hadn't been so pious and boring.'

The anger disappeared as quickly as it had arrived, leaving her sad and disappointed. 'I was a child, Dad. A child you manipulated and blackmailed to suit your own selfish gains.'

'Those selfish gains you're sneering at put you through boarding school, put food in your belly and gave you a front seat to a life most people dream of.'

'You were...*are* a con artist,' she whispered raggedly.

'And you benefitted from the fruits of my labour.' He grinned suddenly, as if the memory brought him paternal pride. 'So does the Sultan know what you did to that poor sucker in Vegas?'

Icy fingers crawled up her spine and latched onto her nape, along with a renewed dose of anger. 'That *man's* name was Bryan. And I didn't do anything to him. He was my friend before *you* ruined everything.'

'Still doesn't answer my question. Does the big man know?'

She blinked back tears, and pursed her lips. 'I haven't divulged every detail of my personal life to him, if that's what you're asking.'

All traces of laughter left his face. 'Because you don't plan on being here that long?'

'I'll be here for your trial.'

'And then what? You'll wait until they lock me up permanently and then wash your hands of me once and for all?' he sneered.

'I don't—'

His chains jangled again as his hand slashed through the air. 'Forget it. Maybe I'll die before any of this happens.'

She inhaled sharply. 'Don't say that!'

'Why not? Maybe expecting you to forget the past was too much to hope for—'

Whatever he'd been about to say was suddenly chopped off by the deep spate of coughing that racked him. The horrendous sound, accompanied by the sound of the rattling chains in jarring synchronicity, went on for almost a minute. And then he lowered his hand.

Three things happened almost simultaneously.

Esme's heart lurched at the bright red smear of blood coating her father's palm.

Her father's eyes caught hers for a moment then began to roll back in his head as his body listed sickeningly to the side.

Zaid walked back into the room, his eyes latching on her as she lunged for her father.

'Esmeralda.'

She barely heeded the taut command in his voice. Barely felt him arrive beside her as she dropped to her knees next to the wheelchair.

'Dad?'

'Step away from him, Esmeralda.'

'No!' Fear climbing into her throat, she placed her hand on his father's cheek. 'Dad!'

He didn't respond.

Zaid spoke sharply in Arabic, and she heard the sound of running feet. 'Esmeralda.'

She shook her head, her gaze fixed on the unmoving form of her father. 'Dad!'

Strong hands gripped her shoulders and pulled her up. Blindly she turned, fisted Zaid's lapels and stared into his grim face. 'I'll give you whatever you want. Please. Just help him!'

CHAPTER SEVEN

THE NEXT WEEK passed at times in a dizzying blur, at times in nerve-racking slow motion.

Her father had received the diagnosis of severe bronchitis and possible pneumonia with a shrug when he finally came round, and his fatalistic attitude seemed to deepen by the minute. Esme, her despair escalating, pleaded with Zaid again. His response after she'd been summoned to his office on her return from the hospital that first night had been bracing, to say the least.

'And what do you expect me to do about it?'

'Something. Anything! Please, Zaid. His lawyer isn't answering his phone calls. I know you're the prosecutor but surely you can make a recommendation for something to be done?'

'Something like what?' he enquired coldly. 'And don't be coy about what you want. I know many conversations have taken place between you and your father at the hospital.'

'I'm not asking for anything that's outside the law. Can't you offer him protective custody or something like that? And before you say he's a criminal, remember he hasn't been tried and found guilty yet. If the rule of law means so much to you, then prove it. Treat him like a human being and help me stop this from happening again.'

Despite the condemning emotions that swirled through his eyes at her outburst, he didn't respond immediately. She knew the tide was about to turn. So far his actions had been those of the ruler of a rich, if somewhat turbulent kingdom. But the ruthless lawyer whose skills had been honed in the glass and chrome power corridors of Washington DC was finally emerging.

He rounded his desk and placed himself squarely before her. 'You wish me to help your father?'

'Yes.'

'Is this where you suggest a *quid pro quo* arrangement? Reiterate your offer to do *anything*?'

The knot of apprehension didn't prevent her from responding. 'If it'll help my father, then yes.'

Again a contemplative silence greeted her question. Then he returned to his desk. 'Very well. You will be informed of the exact details in due course.'

In due course resulted in days of being left in suspense by his absolute silence until her summons today to the house two hours outside Ja'ahr City.

The trip to Jeddebah had been as rough and unforgiving as the terrain surrounding the stunning property in which she now stood, although Esme admitted some parts of it had been raw in their beauty and magnificent to witness.

The mountains, for instance. Green and majestic to the east, they formed a sharp contrast to the distant and endless roll of the desert to the west. Until they dramatically gave way to the turbulent waters of the Persian Gulf. She'd arrived three hours ago at the location on the southernmost point of Ja'ahr half an hour before a security escort had delivered her father.

Esme had been relieved to see his mood dramatically improved, despite the armed guards surrounding him and the menacing-looking security monitor attached to his left ankle. Despite his state, it didn't take long for the healthier-looking Jeffrey Scott to begin subtly owning the place.

A place she'd secured for him at a price she had yet to be fully cognisant of.

She'd been informed of her father's transfer to house arrest by Fawzi this morning, but the Sultan's private secretary had been mute about everything else, including when she would see Zaid again.

But she wasn't going to be kept in the dark for long.

She'd watched the helicopter land on the vast green lawn abutting the sheer cliffs of the house minutes ago. From the west-facing window she'd followed the tall, imposing figure silhouetted against the setting sun as he'd ducked beneath the rotor blades before striking a path for the house. His dark robes flowed dramatically around his head and body as he walked. He went out of sight, and her stomach hollowed. The sensation wasn't acute but it was real and astonishing enough to realise that she'd missed seeing Zaid.

Exhaling in a burst of unnerving disquiet, she frowned as her brain wrestled with the astounding revelation. She was still frozen in place when she sensed his presence. She didn't need to turn around to confirm that those penetrating eyes were on her body. Her spine was tingling, the skin between her shoulders twitching with an awareness she had no hope of suppressing. But still she fought what was happening to her. She had to try. Giving in to even a tiny bit of it would be risking emotions she'd sworn never to dally with again. Letting emotions get the better of her, letting herself be swept away with possibilities of a different life had ended badly the only time she'd allowed someone in.

So she stood at the window, fighting the sensations rampaging through her body with everything she had.

'Are you going to turn around and greet me, Esmeralda?' he drawled in a deep, low voice.

Her stomach dipped and tightened at the way he pronounced her name, the sensuality it evoked. Esme clenched her fists against the feeling, and turned.

'Hello, Za... Your Highness.' She changed her mind over using his given name. It was safer that way. Safer to maintain distance between them.

Keep this straightforward.

Keep it professional.

'Thank you for arranging all this for my father.' She indicated the room, and the house. 'And also for his care at the hospital. I don't know what would've happened if you hadn't been there. So...thank you.'

'Is this finally the frothing of gratitude you promised?' he asked as he stepped deeper into the room, his grace and elegance evoking images of a sleek jungle predator.

The reminder of her waspish words triggered a blush, one she was still fighting when he stopped in front of her. The disparity in their heights forced her head up. Again she was unable to quell the zap of heat that arrowed through her. 'If that is what you wish it to be.'

He remained silent for a stretch before he spoke. 'I would've preferred it not to have been triggered by your father,' he said, his voice containing a bite that produced a different reaction from her. She watched him cast a displeased glance around the room before returning his attention to her. 'I take it he's better pleased with his accommodations?' he drawled.

'Yes, he is.'

Esme wasn't surprised at all when his mouth flattened. 'He orchestrated everything to end up this way. You know this, don't you?' he bit out, his mood darkening further.

Her heart dropped because that same thought had occurred to her. 'Maybe. But the fact remains that his health, not to mention his personal safety, was at risk at the prison.'

The hand he lifted to trace her cheek was gentle but, in direct contrast, the look in his eyes was stark, resigned with more than a trace of bitterness.

Esme swallowed, instinctively shying away from knowing whatever was coming even as her skin heated and tingled at his touch.

'Be that as it may, you've proved me right after all. Nothing comes without a price.'

'But we're both getting what we want. Isn't that all that matters?' Her voice was barely a murmur, his continued caress and their opposing conversation ripping her concentration to shreds.

'Is that how you justify coming to a criminal's aid?' he accused.

Stung, she jerked away from his hand. 'I'm helping him because, criminal or not, he doesn't deserve to be attacked! I'd do the same for anyone else.'

'But you're going over and above for your father, despite knowing exactly what kind of man he is.'

The urge to fold her arms in the universal posture of defence was strong. But she managed to keep her hands at her sides. 'Did you come here merely to condemn me and my father?'

'I came to take you back to the palace. The next stage of our arrangement needs to be hammered out.'

A foreboding little shiver went through her. 'But my father—'

'Will be fine. One of his guards is an army medic. Besides, our agreement doesn't include you remaining here to play nursemaid.'

'What does it include exactly? You haven't yet told me.'

'We will discuss it back at the palace. If you wish to say goodbye to your father, do it now.'

'Did someone mention me?'

Zaid tensed at the intrusion. Then they both turned.

The eyes of a newly shaven, showered and dressed Jeffrey swung from her to Zaid. Then he executed a graceful bow worthy of an award-winning performance. 'Your

Highness, please allow me to express my gratitude for the kindness you have shown me.'

'You have your daughter to thank for this,' Zaid rasped.

Her father straightened and eyed her, the speculative gleam in his eyes intensifying. 'Do I? I hope the cost wasn't too dear. I don't know what I'd do without her.' His gaze returned to Zaid. 'She's the only family I have left, you see.'

Something passed between the two men. Something that made Esme's hackles rise. But then her father smiled and the sensation shifted. 'Are you staying for dinner, Esmeralda?' he asked. 'Your Highness, I would be honoured to have your company too, of course.'

'She's not staying,' Zaid answered for her. 'Neither am I. Remember, Mr Scott, that the only thing that has changed is the location of your incarceration. And this is only temporary. I'm sure you'll also have noticed that there isn't another dwelling for miles and no means of escape. There's a security drone watching the house at all times. Attempt anything foolish and steps will be taken to stop you. As for future dinners with your daughter, that won't be happening any time soon. After today, she will be permitted to visit you as per the usual regulations—once a week, in the middle of the day.'

Her father gave a curt nod. 'Understood, Your Highness.'

Zaid turned to her. 'We're leaving.' The command gave no room for refusal.

Even though a part of her was relieved not to have been forced into a lingering goodbye with her father, Esme was still bristling by the time she settled into the now-familiar seat of the helicopter and they took off.

He shifted in his seat and she jumped when his robe brushed her leg.

'Do you have something to say to me, Esmeralda, or

am I to be given the silent treatment for the whole of the journey?'

She turned her head, then wished she hadn't when she noted just how close he was. 'Did you have to talk to him like that?'

'Like what? A man who doesn't make his living from exploiting weakness in others? Tell me he wasn't seeking to take advantage of the situation and I will offer my regrets.'

She couldn't reply because she couldn't refute the accusation.

Silence fell between them for another ten minutes until she couldn't stand it any longer.

'Whatever he's done, he's still my father. Would you turn your back on yours in my shoes?'

'My father lived an exemplary life of honour and integrity. I would never have needed to make such a sacrifice,' he stated, overwhelming pride stamped in his voice.

But that wasn't what caught Esme's attention. It was his use of the past tense. 'Lived?' she asked, the thought occurring to her that although she knew he'd inherited the throne after his uncle's death from a heart attack, she hadn't come across any information about his parents in her brief research. Come to think of it, information on Zaid's own childhood and teenage years had been very sparse. Only his early professional life and later accomplishments had been documented.

She glanced at him at his continued silence and only then noticed the tension that gripped him. Even before he spoke, Esme knew something huge was coming. 'My father has been dead for a very long time,' he said.

Her chest tightened in sympathy. 'And your mother?'

His mouth compressed, dispersing the momentary flash of pain she glimpsed in his face. 'They perished together.'

Her earlier admonition to herself to stay away from personal subjects replayed in her mind, only to be ignored. 'How did they die?'

In the semi-darkness of the helicopter, his face settled into ragged, haunted lines. 'They were assassinated by my uncle as we drove home from my thirteenth birthday celebrations.'

Shock held her rigid for several seconds. 'Oh, Zaid... My God. I'm... I don't know what to say!'

'In such circumstances there rarely are adequate words,' he replied.

'I shouldn't have pried in the first place,' she returned, horrified at churning up bad memories for him.

He shrugged offhandedly, although the eyes that probed hers were an intense dark bronze. 'You have me wide open, Esmeralda. Ask your questions and I will answer them.'

The distinctive American term reminded her where he'd grown up. 'Did you go to the States after...after what happened to your parents?'

'I couldn't stay here. Not unless I wished to invite another attempt on my life.'

She gasped. 'You mean your uncle intended you to be killed too?'

'He had his eye on the throne. That meant doing away with everyone who stood in his way, including the boy who would grow to be the man with the rightful claim to the throne. He'd meant to have us all killed that night. My father shielded me with his body and his aides managed to raise the alarm before Khalid's men could finish the job properly.'

The matter-of-fact way he relayed the tale didn't stop her from seeing the pain in his eyes.

'What...what happened after that?'

'Khalid's hands were tied. He couldn't very well execute a child without incurring the wrath of his people, even though everyone knew how he'd become Sultan. Some things are unforgivable. I was delivered to my maternal grandmother and given safe passage out of Ja'ahr on condition that we would never return, and a murderer and despot took power and ruled Ja'ahr for twenty years. The rest, as they say, is history.'

For several minutes, she absorbed the stomach-turning news, a few pennies beginning to drop.

'That's why you became a lawyer, isn't it? To put criminals like your uncle behind bars? Perhaps to challenge his rule when the time came?'

A bitter smile cracked his lips, but it was gone in the next instant. 'I dedicated every day of my life after I was tossed out of the only home I'd ever known to honing judicial weapons that would right the wrongs done to my parents and to me. Except Khalid had the audacity to succumb to his excessive indulgences and die of a heart attack caused by a clogged artery before I got the chance to see justice done.'

The cold observation sent a shiver through her. So did the stark confirmation of why Zaid was a formidable opponent to have. The harrowing wrongs done to him as a child, and to his people in the years following, was the reason some viewed him as a ruthless ruler now. It was also the reason he didn't trust anyone.

But most of all, Esme knew, staring at him, that it was the reason he could never find out about her past. Those few weeks with Bryan and how everything had ended would never be struck from her copybook, no matter whose fault it had been. She didn't know what would happen to her father during his trial, but she instinctively knew that the reluctant concession Zaid had granted her father would be withdrawn the second he found out.

Unease whispered up her spine at the thought of discovery. And this time not even reminding herself that she was no longer that person could wash away that sensation.

But still she met his gaze, infused truth into her words. 'I'm sorry,' she said again. 'I didn't mean to drag all of this up for you.'

'Curiosity is a natural occurrence when swimming in the getting-to-know-you waters, at least on the part of women, is it not?'

The tiny mocking voice inside her head that irked her for wanting to know just how many women he'd *got to know* was smothered in favour of a much more persistent and powerful emotion. One that had her shifting sideways, the better to see his face, she told herself. What she didn't account for was her hand disobeying her brain to slide over the seat and come to rest on top of his. 'As is sympathy. I'm sorry for your loss.' Her voice was a husky murmur, reflecting her lingering regret at bringing up memories that must be hard for him to recall.

Zaid didn't answer. Instead his gaze dropped to the pale hand she'd placed over his brown one. To the fingers starting to tremble as that blasted, ever-present hyperawareness thickened in the space between them.

Still without speaking, he turned his hand over, splaying it open until his larger palm was pressed firmly against hers, dominating her small one. Heat singed their touching flesh as acutely as if a naked flame had been held against it. The sight of their clasped hands shouldn't have been so basely erotic. But it was.

He moved, sliding his skin more firmly against hers. Esme gasped as the sensation lodged low in her belly, then unfurled throughout her body, concentrating with shameless urgency between her thighs.

She dragged her gaze up a breathless second before she realised his intention. She had time to move, time to duck her head or vocalise her denial. But she didn't draw away. Because she didn't want to.

She stayed put, breath strangled to nothing, as Zaid slid his fingers through the loose knot of her hair and drew her firmly, inexorably, towards his kiss.

Just like the man, the kiss was unapologetically dominant, his mouth owning hers the moment they touched. He tasted of Ja'ahrian coffee and an elusive spice. He tasted like all the forbidden desires she'd sworn off years ago. But the formidable man who'd already taken up far too much room in her head was impossible to deny.

Hot, hungry, and intent on conquering her, Zaid pressed her back against the seat, angled his lips for a better fit and charged through her feeble defences.

Within seconds, her lips were parting beneath the possessive pressure of his, letting him in when he demanded entry. The slow, glorious slide of his tongue against her lower inner lip elicited a moan she couldn't have suppressed if she'd tried. As if the sound pleased him, he repeated it again and again, before catching her plump lip between his teeth. The nip of his teeth sent sparks racing through her system. She was chasing that unfamiliar strain of delight when he delved deeper between her lips. This time, his tongue slid boldly against hers. Pleasure arrowed straight between her legs, plumping up her most sensitive flesh, turning her slick with shockingly demanding need as the fingers in her hair drew her even closer.

On a desperate whimper that echoed through the enclosed space, Esme opened even wider for him, the hand lying against his on the seat shifting to grip him tighter. Zaid gave a thick groan, then meshed his fingers through hers. He brought their clasped hands up between them, then pressed his body against hers.

The feel of his heart beating against her hand, hers beating against his, caused something to lurch alarmingly inside her. Reluctant to explore why in that moment, she chose a different type of exploration. With her free hand, she slid her fingers over one strong bicep. Sleek muscles immediately rippled beneath her touch. Emboldened, she caressed upward, over the broad curve of his shoulder, to the neck opening of his robe. At the first brush of her fingers against his bare nape, Zaid muttered a thick, foreign imprecation. The sound was smashed between them as his kiss took on a frenzied, bone-melting intimacy. Something jolted inside her again. Only she realised a moment later that the movement wasn't just inside her.

The sound of the pilot's door sliding open announced their arrival back at the Royal Palace. She jerked back from Zaid, then pushed frantically at his muscled chest when he didn't budge. His fingers convulsed in her hair for a charged second before he drew back. But although he sat back in his seat, his hand held hers for another moment, his gaze tracking over her face with blatant hunger before he released her.

'Come. We will continue this inside,' he instructed in a rough, hoarse voice, then lifted his hand in a signal to his guards.

The notion that he just expected her to fall into his lap...or his bed, struck a fiery nerve, but, with the usual clutch of staff accompanying them, she had no choice but to swallow her irritation as she walked silently at his side.

Lost in her ire, Esme didn't realise where they were until the scents of mouth-watering spices and cooked meat hit her nostrils. Surprised and curiously out of sorts, she glanced around the dining room.

'We're having dinner?' she asked the moment his ever-present entourage were dismissed and they were alone.

Faint amusement drifted over his features, although his eyes retained a turbulent heat and his body a banked tension that suggested he was still caught in the throes of what had happened in the helicopter.

'Did you think that I intended to whisk you straight into my bed and have my way with you?' he drawled.

Heat flared up to stain her cheeks at his accurate reading of her thoughts. All the same, she raised her chin. 'You say that as if it would've been a foregone conclusion.'

He sauntered towards her, removing his *keffiyeh* and tossing it on a nearby surface. His outer robe followed, leaving him in only his muscle-skimming tunic and trousers. With his magnificent body on display, Esme couldn't fault his powerful animal grace, the lithe movement effortlessly trapping her attention, capturing both her mind and body.

She held her breath as he reached out, lazily, assuredly, and trailed his thumb over the mouth he'd kissed so thoroughly barely fifteen minutes ago. The mouth he eyed hungrily for a long moment, before his gaze met hers.

'I am not ashamed to admit that I desire you, Esmeralda. You captivate me. What took place a little earlier tells me the feeling is mutual. Where that captivation takes us is a destination I intend to thoroughly enjoy exploring.' His voice was full of erotic promise, of heady delights that had her body throbbing anew, setting off sensual fires that thrilled and terrified her.

It was the latter emotion that had her stepping back. 'It won't take us anywhere,' she blurted, as much out of the need to spell it out for herself as it was for him.

Pure male arrogance blazed from his eyes. When his gaze dropped to her lips again, it was all she could do not to tug the still tingling flesh into her mouth. 'Are you sure about that?' he challenged, his voice low, laced with sensual danger.

Alarm growing, Esme took another step back. 'Yes, I'm

sure. What happened tonight was a mistake. Rest assured, it won't happen again.'

It seemed almost superhuman, the way he concisely eradicated every vestige of arousal from his face. It didn't happen immediately, so she had time to wonder why her disappointment was so cutting, why she was already mourning something she'd rejected so definitively.

CHAPTER EIGHT

It took a considerable amount of effort to lock her knees to stay put as his hand dropped.

'Very well. But we still need to discuss the flip side of our arrangement,' he said, his tone brisk as he spun on his heel and walked to the head of the table. 'We'll do that while we eat. Unless you object to dinner too?' he threw over his shoulder.

'No, dinner is fine,' she said, scrambling to gather her wits.

She followed at a slower pace, properly taking in her surroundings for the first time. This dining room was different from where she'd shared breakfast with him a week ago. It was also different from where she herself had eaten her meals every day for the last week.

'Where are we? I mean, which part of the palace?' she asked when they were seated at the table.

'In my private wing.'

Which included his bedroom, she concluded on a dizzy, unwelcome thought. Were they, even now, a stone's throw from where Zaid slept? And did he sleep alone? It was the first time Esme had given herself permission to dwell on just who shared the enigmatic Sultan's bed. But now that she'd made it clear she had no intention of falling into his bed, her brain couldn't let go of wondering just who he would invite there instead.

She hadn't seen signs of it because she'd been preoccupied with other things, namely her father, but did the Ja'ahrian Royal Palace, as with most Sultanates, possess a harem?

The strong urge to ask hovered on her tongue. She bit

back the impulse and helped herself to the platter of fragrant couscous served with salad and an assortment of sliced meats. From previous meals, she knew the meats had been slow roasted for hours with honey, spices and nuts. The promise of the melt-in-your-mouth offering reminded her she hadn't eaten since breakfast.

'That isn't too much of an inconvenience for you, I hope?' he said blandly, and she realised he'd been watching her, waiting for a reaction to his answer.

'Not at all,' she offered boldly.

The twitch of his lips told her he didn't entirely believe her. But he didn't contradict her.

They ate the first course in silence, the uneasy tension building until chewing and swallowing each morsel of the delicious food became a chore.

'As of this afternoon, I have recused myself as your father's prosecutor.'

It was the last thing she'd expected him to say. But once absorbed, the statement should have brought relief. Instead, her senses tingled with a not so terrifying warning. 'Why?'

'I want there to be no conflict of interest arising from my association with you.'

'But...we have no association.'

Brandy-coloured eyes gleamed for a moment before his lashes swept his expression away. 'Not yet. But that is going to change soon, I think.'

For some reason, her breath strangled in her lungs. 'Even though our association will be strictly professional?'

He stared at her for a moment before his gaze dropped again, and Esme got the uncanny feeling he was keeping something from her. 'Even so.'

'Um, okay. Who will take your place?'

'That is for my attorney general to decide. He will present me with his recommendations at the end of this week.'

Before she could ask further questions, two butlers entered. She remained silent as their plates were whisked away, and just as efficiently dessert platters were set on the table before the servers were dismissed.

The creations were too exquisite to resist, even though Esme doubted she would be able to do them justice. Nevertheless, she helped herself to dates stuffed with goats' cheese and sprinkled with sugar, butter biscuits topped with Ja'ahrian yoghurt, and sweet dumplings topped with honey and ground pistachios.

'Touch Global have a base here in Ja'ahr,' he said without preamble the moment they were alone again.

Her nape tingled in premonition as she sampled a dumpling. 'I wasn't aware of that.'

'They weren't encouraged in their social work programme in my kingdom until recently,' he expanded.

He meant until after Khalid Al-Ameen's death and Zaid's ascension to the throne. The realisation that the dilapidated state of his kingdom was down to his uncle and not to Zaid hit home with brute force. Everything she'd accused him of during her TV interview came back to bite her hard. The fish had indeed rotted from the head down, but it had been a different head altogether.

'And that's what you want in repayment for what you did for my father? For me to work with Touch Global's branch here in Ja'ahr?' she asked.

He didn't answer immediately. Instead, he picked up a stuffed date and popped it into his mouth. The act of watching another person chew shouldn't have been so engrossing. And yet Esme couldn't look away from the tight jaw, the shadowed cheek or the sexy mouth that had possessed her own so expertly.

He swallowed and her breathing settled. Until she saw the brooding look in his eyes as he stared at her. 'No. I have decided to utilise your expertise in another way.'

The tingling on her nape increased. 'How?'

'You will be my personal liaison to the organisation.'

She tried not to dwell on the word *personal*. 'I... What does that mean?'

'In the next few weeks I'll be touring some of the more...out of the way parts of Ja'ahr. Touch Global are getting a handle on which communities are most needy here in Ja'ahr City and the surrounding areas. Much more help is needed in remote areas. You'll travel with me, assess the needs of the people, then report to Touch. Based on your recommendations, they'll ensure the necessary infrastructure is put in place.'

As positions went, it was an exciting one, even if a huge leap from what she did back in London. But the prospect of working that closely with Zaid made her go hot. And then cold. When the butterflies in her belly finally settled midway between the two points, she cleared her throat.

'I'm not sure that I can take the position for the whole length of time it will take for my father's trial to happen but I'll request an extension of my leave...' She trailed to a stop when his brooding eyes narrowed on her.

'This isn't a negotiation, Esmeralda. This is where I list my demands and you confirm in the vein of the "I'll give you whatever you want" you promised to me last week. Unless that was an empty promise?' he queried, his voice deceptively soft.

Esme had come to realise that was his most deadly tone.

Mouth dry, she hurried to speak. 'It wasn't empty, but I still have to ask—'

'Your employer has agreed to a transfer of your services, effective immediately, for as long as I want you,' he supplied in an authoritarian voice.

She froze in her chair. 'What? How...? You had no right to do that!'

'Why not?' he demanded haughtily.

'Because...because...'

'You wanted to do it in your own precious time?' he suggested when she sputtered. 'Did I not tell you I would inform you of the details in due course?'

'Details of what you wanted from me, not details of how you'd taken over my life!'

'I had no wish to waste time on unnecessary arguments like the one we're having right now. Besides, you forget I have experience in the corporate world. Asking your boss for an indefinable amount of leave wouldn't have gone down well. Not without divulging a more comprehensive reason as to why you were in Ja'ahr in the first place. I take it you didn't tell him about your father the first time around?' he asked, although his droll tone suggested he already knew the answer.

Esme's stomach dipped lower, her anger at his high-handedness taking a temporary back seat to his unerring reasoning. 'You...you didn't tell him, did you?'

'Since the call wasn't of a personal nature, no, I didn't.'

'So he agreed, just like that?' she pressed.

'Yes, Esmeralda. Just like that. But I dare say receiving a call from the Sultan of a notable kingdom isn't an everyday occurrence and he went the extra mile to treat it as such.'

'You mean you threw your weight around and got the results you wanted.'

'Of course,' he agreed smoothly. 'Although there wasn't much throwing needed. He will have the privilege of adding my kingdom to his portfolio of clients, and my promise of a personal recommendation should you do a good job was just the extra incentive he needed.' A hard, implacable look settled over his face, along with a trace of the hunger she thought he'd completely eradicated. 'So now your way has been cleared, do I have your agreement that you'll stay for as long as I need you?'

Esme fought against the distinct sensation that she'd

been well and truly cornered. And not for the purpose of serving as Zaid's liaison. There was stealth about him, a deeper purpose brewing behind his eyes that wouldn't allow the tightening in her stomach to ease. But how could she fight it when she didn't know what it was? Especially when in the face of what he'd said, what he'd done for her father, and what he was striving to do for his people, she could only give him one answer?

'Yes, I'll stay.'

In the moment before she answered, Zaid went through a half a dozen rebuttals in preparation for a negative response. Her inner battle had been plain to see on her face. So it took a moment or two before he realised she'd agreed. He absorbed her words with a relief he hadn't been expecting to feel. The punch of elation that followed on its heels was equally perturbing and irritating, considering he'd mentally slammed the door on the possibility of any future sexual interaction with her.

Zaid wasn't arrogant in thinking he could change her mind about her decision should he wish to. Esmeralda Scott was a desirable woman, and their brief interlude had spiked a hunger in his blood that he was still struggling with. He'd also seen her quickly hidden disappointment after his acceptance of her bold denial of their mutual chemistry.

But mixing business with pleasure rarely ended well. And he had enough people questioning his motives with her as it was, especially in light of the strings he'd pulled this week on behalf of her father.

No, he would be better off finding a discreet alternative avenue for slaking his lust. Except the thought of doing just that only increased his irritation. That and the reminder of why she was in his kingdom in the first place.

'Good.' His tone was much curter than necessary. The widening of her alluring eyes and the stiffening of her lush body told him so. But his patience was ebbing. 'Fawzi will provide you with an itinerary in the morning.'

She carried on staring at him for a moment before her gaze dropped. 'Okay. Um... I'll say goodnight, then.'

He rose and pulled back her chair, and noticed her faint surprise at the gesture. 'You have a problem with a little chivalry?'

She shook her head, and the already precarious knot of hair threatened to emancipate itself. The reminder of how soft and silky the tresses had felt between his fingers threatened another bout of hunger. Directing a silent, pithy curse at his libido did nothing to alleviate the growing ache.

'Not a problem, no, just a little surprised, that's all.'

He allowed himself a tiny smile. 'My grandmother, may she rest in peace, would turn in her grave if she thought for a moment that I'd abandoned my manners.'

Her answering smile was equally brief, but the transformation of her features from beautiful to enchanting made his grip tight on the back of her chair. 'Were you two very close?'

Zaid told himself all he would allow was a single breath of her cherry blossom and jasmine scent as she fell into step beside him and they left his dining room. But in the next breath he was sampling her alluring perfume again, wondering where the shampoo smell ended and the jasmine and feminine scent began. He pulled his focus back to what she'd asked him with aggravating effort.

'Despite our exile, she was determined to raise me as if I was a ruler in waiting. Besides my normal studies, I had to learn every single Ja'ahrian custom and law, excel in matters of diplomacy, and, of course, the correct table manners. She was a hard taskmistress, but she was also soft and maternal when it mattered.'

'I'm glad,' she murmured.

Something in her voice made him glance at her. He caught a trace of sadness before she attempted to reinstate that air of rigid control around herself. For some reason he couldn't fathom in that moment, he wanted to smash through it, leave the true Esmeralda Scott exposed. He was sure it was that notion that prompted his next question.

'When did you lose your mother?'

Wary tension stiffened her spine. 'How did you know?'

He steered her down another hallway, one he knew would be quieter at that time of night. 'Your father said you were the only family he had.'

The tiniest wave of relief washed over her face. 'Oh... yes.' She pretended an interest in a nearby sculpture of a warrior on a horse as she gathered herself. 'My mother died when I was fourteen. But she wasn't in my life by then. They divorced when I was thirteen and she moved to Australia.'

Zaid frowned. 'So then it was just your father and you?'

The wariness encroached again. 'Yes.'

'It won't come as a surprise to you that I did my homework on your father. He has been...active in a number of countries for a while now. Unless you were left in the care of others, I assume you were with him?'

Her laugh was a little strained. 'What is this, an interrogation? I thought you were no longer my father's prosecutor?'

'You fault me for wishing to know better the woman who will be working for me?' Perhaps his tactics were unfair. Perhaps he needed to leave the subject alone. But, seeing her drag her lower lip between her teeth as she weighed up his question, Zaid felt that insanely strong urge to destroy her defences once more. He wanted to know her, wanted to find out what made her strong and wary and bold and vulnerable.

'I guess not.' He watched her consider her words carefully before responding. 'No, I wasn't left the in the care of others. I was in boarding school during term time, then I got a chance to see the world during school holidays with my father. It was a great adventure.'

The glossy veneer she tried to throw on her childhood sent a pulse of anger through him. 'If it was all so great, why have you been estranged from your father for the past eight years?'

He saw the shock his question brought. Then her stunning eyes narrowed. 'This feels awfully like an interrogation.'

'Perhaps you were ashamed of the man he was and wished to distance yourself from him?' he pressed.

'Or have you considered the possibility that we just came to a time in our lives where we needed to go our separate ways? Like most children do when they come of age, I wanted to spread my wings. I wanted a…career, so I returned home to England.'

She was lying. Or at the very least not telling the whole truth. Zaid frowned at the pang of unnerving disquiet at the revelation and wondered at it. He'd stopped being surprised by the actions of others a long time ago.

So why this woman's half-truths should disturb him so deeply, why it should tap into a well of disappointment he'd thought had dried up a long time ago, surprised him. Enough to make him quicken his footsteps towards her suite.

'Zaid…um… Your Highness?'

He whirled back, her reversion to using his title just one more irritant in the giant cluster of irritants she represented in his life.

He watched her stumble back from him and clawed back his control. 'What is it?' he asked.

In the lamplit softness of the corridor, her face was both

enthralling and wary, although she held his gaze boldly. 'I… I think I can find my way from here.'

He checked out his surroundings, noted they were a few corridors away from where she slept. 'I'll see you to your door,' he stated imperiously, then resumed walking.

She walked by his side in silence for the rest of the way. When they reached her suite, he pushed the double doors open.

Aisha and Nashwa turned at their entrance. At the sight of their Sultan both women dropped into low curtsies with softly lyrical greetings.

Zaid responded, and moments later both women were rushing away. When the doors closed behind them, Esme glanced at him.

'I know women in Ja'ahr aren't chaperoned as strictly as in other countries, but should I have been consulted as to whether I want to be gossiped about for having the Sultan in my bedroom at this time of night?'

'They will be back shortly. Had I harboured other motives, I would've dismissed them for the night,' he said, heat rising in his groin as thoughts of just such a scenario embedded themselves in his mind.

A blush crept into her cheeks. Zaid wanted to trace the creamy pink skin with his fingers. The memory of its softness bit into him with a savage hunger still puzzling to him.

'So what are your motives, besides triggering tongues to start wagging about me?'

'Tongues will not wag about you in that way. In Ja'ahr, a woman isn't punished for desiring a man, neither is she expected to have a chaperone guarding her virtue, unless she requests it. Women's rights are respected, and they are free to champion their own integrity once they come of age.'

'I'm pleased to hear that.'

'Good, so no one will condemn you for entertaining me in your suite.'

She inhaled sharply. 'But I'm not entertaining you here. And you could've said goodnight to me at the door.'

Her forthright manner, unlike everyone else who treated him deferentially, made the blood thrum faster through his veins. 'Perhaps it's that captivation I spoke about that keeps me here. Perhaps I wish to mark you as mine despite...'

Her eyes rounded, her breath growing visibly short. 'Despite?'

'Despite the instinctive warning that I should keep away from you.'

'Maybe you should heed the warning. Think of the gossip.'

'There will always be interest in what the King of Ja'ahr does and who he does it with. Will such attention bother you?'

Her tongue darted out to lick her lower lip. It took a considerable amount of willpower not to lower his head and taste her right then and there.

'Why are we talking about this?' she asked, her own gaze dropping to his mouth.

Lust and impatience prowled through him. 'You really need to ask? When you can hardly breathe for all the hunger threatening to consume us right now?'

Her breath audibly caught. The predator in him enjoyed that sound immensely. 'Zaid, I thought we agreed that there would be nothing—'

'Tell me you don't want me and I will leave,' he cut her off, unwilling to be reminded of what he'd so readily accepted earlier tonight.

'I...' She stopped, shook her head. 'This is a bad idea.'

He cupped her shoulders, felt her soft warm skin beneath the thin cotton of her dress. Hunger pounded harder. 'It's not the confirmation I requested. Admit how you feel and tell me you want me, Esmeralda. Or do you imagine a lie would be easier?'

A vein of hurt passed through her eyes. Despite her fixed stare, her mouth trembled for a telling second before she curbed the weakness. 'I don't lie.'

He brushed the hurt and the response aside, as he did with the reminder that even if she didn't lie, she still hadn't told him the complete truth about her past during their conversation earlier. 'Then tell me what I want to know.'

She looked cornered, defeated for a wild second. Then that defiant little chin rose. 'Fine! I want you. But I still think this is a bad—'

He slanted his mouth over hers, kissing the words that held undeniable truth in them from her delectable mouth. And just like that, the fuse of desire leapt high and became all-consuming. Zaid clasped her tighter to him, moulded her lissom body to his until her softness was pressed against his hardness. And still he wanted her closer. As if she felt the same, her hands rose to slide around his waist. Soft, velvety lips opened beneath his. He delved with an eagerness that bordered on the uncouth. But he didn't care. Her responsiveness, the little moans she gave at the back of her throat each time their tongues met, triggered the headiest sensation he'd ever experienced. But even as he deepened the kiss, Zaid knew there was more in store. He knew and he hungered for it.

It was what drew his fingers to tunnel through her hair, disposing of the handful of pins that secured the loose knot. Honey-gold strands tumbled over his fingers in a fall of glorious silk. Suffused in her wild feminine scent, he caressed her scalp, tightened his hold on her and pulled her even closer. The unmistakeable feeling of her belly cradling his erection was a thousand highs distilled into one glorious sensation.

The hands wrapped around his waist splayed over his

back, her fingers exploring, digging, sending him wild as she strained and whimpered against him. Mouths devouring each other, Zaid walked them backwards until the arm of the nearest sofa halted their progress. Expertly manoeuvring them, he sank down and pulled her into his lap without breaking the kiss. Still keeping her prisoner against him, he tasted her, deeper, longer, until their frantic breathing echoed lustily through the room. Zaid was aware he was getting carried away, that the servants he'd so cavalierly dismissed were hovering right outside the double doors.

But still he slid his hand from her hip and up her side to rest beneath the sweet curve of one full breast.

Her breath caught. He broke the kiss long enough to voice what he couldn't keep silent. 'You're like a lush oasis after a long exile in the desert, *jamila*,' before he sealed his lips to hers once more. Her long, helpless moan drove his hand up.

Firm, gorgeous, magnificent, he gloried in the weight of her full breast before sliding his thumb over the engorged peak. The beautiful little jerk she gave powered his arousal higher. Then, unable to resist the clarion call, he pulled down the elastic neckline of her dress. Zaid kissed her for a moment longer before the other temptation grew too much to resist. The straining pink tip of her nipple was visible through the delicate white lace covering her. With fingers that trembled with the force of his desire he tugged the material out of the way. The strangled sound she made in her throat drew his gaze up. Flushed. Breathless. Beautiful.

He deliberately kept their gazes locked as he lowered his head and drew her nipple into his mouth. Watched her lovely eyes darken with drowning desire before her eyelids began to flutter. Gripped with the need to witness even more of her pleasure, he flicked his tongue over her peak, again and again, then repeated it with the twin. Only when the heat coursing through his body threatened to rage completely out of control did he finally lift his head.

'Ambrosia, *habiba*,' he muttered roughly. 'You taste like pure, heavenly ambrosia.'

Her answer was to slide her hand over his nape and tug his head back down to her. With a ragged chuckle that spoke of his own unstoppable desire, he tossed himself headlong back into the drugging power of her body.

He was well and truly lost in it when she started to murmur something. With the scent of her arousal joining the maelstrom of powerful elixirs surrounding them, he didn't realise she was calling to him urgently until she began to push frantically at his shoulders.

'Zaid, stop!'

'Not yet,' he responded thickly. His other hand had left her hair a long time ago, and both hands now cupped the glorious globes of her breasts. He was nowhere near ready to relinquish his prize.

'Please!'

The frantic plea finally impinged on his senses. A deep but highly unsatisfying breath later, he drew back. And finally heard the sound of cautious knocking. He was glad she didn't understand his language as he issued a crude, pithy curse and reluctantly let her go.

She got the gist, though. Her face flamed as she hurriedly straightened her clothes and tumbled off his lap. She swayed slightly as she regained her feet. Zaid caught her hips and steadied her as he attempted to pin down his own runaway control.

Her shoes had come off at some point during their torrid interlude. In her bare feet, her face flushed and her hair in disarray, she was a deliciously petite morsel, one he knew he wouldn't be able to resist devouring in the very near future.

He couldn't stem the growl of anticipation that rose in his throat at the thought. She shifted beneath his hold, her agitated gaze darting to the door.

'Be calm. They will not come in until I give permission,' he reassured her gruffly.

Her teeth mangled her swollen bottom lip. 'Then give it,' she urged in a rushed whisper. 'Before they think you're...that we're...' She pressed her lips together as another blush deepened her colour.

'Making love? Get used to saying the words, Esmeralda, because it is going to happen. The next time I have you in my arms I won't stop at tasting those tempting lips and gorgeous breasts. When I have you in my bed, I won't stop until I possess you, thoroughly and completely.'

Her shaky inhalation drew his gaze back to her chest. Already he craved another taste. He rose to his feet, bent down and brushed her lips with his, gratified when she clung to him for a second. Then he forced himself to release her. Step back.

'Our journey begins early tomorrow. Be ready.'

CHAPTER NINE

THE NEXT TIME I have you in my arms...

For some stupid, sleep-depriving reason, Esme had assumed those words carried with them a very imminent time stamp.

She'd spent the next several nights after their departure from Ja'ahr City and the Royal Palace vacillating between the urge to give in and reiterating stern warnings of why she couldn't. Every night in the breath-taking beauty of her surroundings, be it in a camp made up of giant Bedouin tents or a hut in a desert village as they travelled north towards the oil fields that were the life blood of Ja'ahr, was spent wondering if that would be the night Zaid made his move.

Before she knew it, three weeks had passed.

Three weeks, when he'd treated her like a respected member of his travelling staff, each night reading the detailed reports she'd made on the social care needs of the communities they'd visited and peppering her with questions on points she'd made as they'd shared a simple dinner in the community tent or a mini-banquet in a chieftain's dining room, depending on which host they'd been blessed to spend the evening with.

Each night she'd retreated to her sleeping quarters with Nashwa and Aisha as her constant companions. The two had proved themselves invaluable sources of information, with Nashwa acting as an informal translator when needed. Esme had even learned to accept the presence of the two bodyguards who shadowed her at all times.

Had she not been thoroughly enjoying her new role, Esme was sure she would have gone completely out her mind. But the joy she'd gained from knowing she was making a difference went a long way towards helping her sleep at night, despite being dogged by thoughts of Zaid.

Because it wasn't as if Zaid had lost interest in her. Many times, she'd looked up from a conversation with a matriarch of a community, or a group of teenagers, to find his intense gaze on her. At those times, the depth of his hunger had been plain to see, although those long, lush eyelashes would all too soon sweep away the glimpse into his emotions as he returned to whatever conversation he was engrossed in.

The breathless yearning those looks left behind would leave her feeling needy and bereft for hours, a part of her hating him for eliciting such a devastating craving, and the other part admonishing herself for falling beneath his spell in the first place.

It wasn't surprising therefore then that she was feeling irritable as the sun set on another glorious day on their second night in Tujullah. The northernmost settlement of Ja'ahr was little more than a desert encampment, although the permanent tents were huge and contained an assortment of rooms.

As usual, she'd been allotted her own tent far from the one Zaid occupied—she knew that because she'd watched him disappear with Fawzi into his twenty minutes ago after he'd grilled her on her latest report. Her answers had grown increasingly short until he'd looked up from the document, his narrow-eyed gaze piercing hers before he'd dismissed her and conducted a terse conversation of his own with his personal secretary.

Normally, she would have lingered in the middle of the encampment where groups of men played musical instruments or engaged in heated discussions about the state of the world at large. Tonight, she'd chosen to take a long, relaxing bath in the privacy of her tent. Aisha had looked slightly put out after she'd filled the bath and Esme had dismissed her for the night but she hadn't thought it fair to visit her bad mood on the young girl.

So now she drew the soft sponge filled with jasmine-and-rosewater-scented water over her arm and absently watched the water sparkle in the light of the two dozen candles within the room. In four days they would be returning to Ja'ahr, remaining there for a fortnight before they made another trek east. Zaid had other matters of state to deal with, including a few court cases. Their return would also give her another chance to visit her father. She'd flown back by helicopter for her once weekly visit with him. Although their conversation had got increasingly terse after he'd tried to pry into her relationship with Zaid, she'd promised to return. All she had to do was remind herself that he no longer had any power over her.

She would also be able to liaise with Touch Global about her recommendations for the communities she'd assessed.

But tonight she couldn't concentrate on any of that. Her thoughts were fully centred on Zaid. On whether he'd changed his mind about having her, and why the thought that he might have made her gut clench with such keen disappointment. She was still grappling with those frustratingly divergent thoughts when she left the bath an hour later. Although she yearned for the oblivion of eventual sleep, it was too early to head to bed.

After spending mindless minutes brushing her hair, Esme tugged a lilac-coloured floor-length tunic over her head. Made of the softest silk with delicate gold embroidery at the wide cuffs and hem, the material whispered over her body with silken seduction, drawing a pleasured sigh from her before she grimaced at herself. It was true that she was falling in love with all things Ja'ahr, including the new wardrobe that Zaid had informed her via Nashwa was part of her welcome package. Esme didn't deny the new clothes helped her blend in better and gave her an extra boost of confidence in her new role.

She freed her hair from the collar, tying it into a loose knot at her nape before slipping her feet into matching Arabian slippers. A pair of simple gold chandelier earrings she'd bought at a bazaar two weeks ago and the glide of peach gloss over her lips rounded off her attire.

She was arranging a white scarf over her head when Aisha entered.

Surprised that she'd returned, Esme turned around, ready to gently dismiss her again. But the young girl curtsied shyly.

'Pardon me for the intrusion, Madam, but Fawzi Suleiman is here to see you.'

'Oh...okay.'

Aisha gave a quick nod and dashed back outside. A moment later Fawzi stepped into the tent. He hovered respectfully in the doorway, his fingers in a steeple in front of him.

'His Highness requests your presence, Miss Scott.'

Esme cursed the wild leap of her heart and bit back the strong urge to tell the unfortunate messenger where to tell His Highness to stick his request. She didn't think she could stand another roasting over her meticulous reports. Not to mention the prospect of her current heart rate soaring even higher in Zaid's presence.

'If you would be so kind.' He stepped back and made that elegant inviting gesture with his hand that was nevertheless subtly insistent.

She pursed her lips even as her feet moved towards the large black tent set apart from the rest of the dwellings. Unlike her own, the large opening was barred by a secondary wall of cured leather a few feet from the first, with the entrance to the tent on either side of that taut wall.

She followed Fawzi through the right entrance, and immediately stepped onto the first of a dozen priceless Persian rugs. The royal blue and gold theme of his palace was repeated in the immense cushions bordered by large cylindrical ones that served as a seating area, with dozens of smaller cushions tossed over the floor in sumptuous invitation.

Lit by a giant chandelier of candles hanging from the centre point in the ceiling, the living area was illuminated further by intricately carved Moroccan lanterns hung on various posts inside the tent. There was a smaller grouping of cushions in the centre of which was laid a large platter of fruits and nuts.

Esme took in all of this in seconds, before her senses and gaze zeroed in on the man rising lithely to his feet from the largest divan-like cushion.

A curt nod from him dismissed Fawzi. When his gaze returned to her, his eyes glowed an intense topaz in the light.

She hated the way her breath caught anew. So much she locked her knees to keep her in place. 'You wanted to see me?'

He advanced, a powerful being draped in a rich wine-red tunic, trousers and robe. He wasn't wearing his headgear, and his jet-black hair gleamed under the lamplight. 'You look…irritated,' he observed almost lazily.

But she wasn't fooled. There was a coiled tension within him that sent her pulse racing faster.

'Do I?' she replied. 'It must be because I was planning to go for an evening stroll before I was summoned here.'

A ghost of a smile whispered over his lips. Lips that had possessed hers with such bone-melting mastery. Lips she'd yearned for in her dreams and in her wakeful hours.

'Or perhaps you're feeling a little neglected?'

'Not at all. I'm doing the job I'm here to do. I've seen you every day to make my report. I'm constantly surrounded by Nashwa and Aisha. Oh, and my personal body-guards. Let's not forget them,' she tagged on waspishly.

'The guards are here for your safety.'

'Are they? It's all a little OTT, if you ask me. I mean, each guest having a staff? What's that all about?'

A little of his indolence evaporated. 'There used to be five to a guest, half of whom were given three meals a day and nothing else in the form of a salary. The two members of staff assigned to you now earn enough to be able to feed and clothe their families.'

Contrition bit hard. 'Oh... I didn't know that. And the other three? Are they now on the unemployment line?'

He turned away and led her to the seat he'd just vacated. One of the things she'd learned in the past three weeks was how to sit on floor divans. She sank down sideways, and propped herself up with two cushions, noting too late that Zaid was doing the same. But in her direction.

Within one heartbeat and the next they were a mere foot apart. The slightly shaky breath she took infused her senses with his powerfully evocative scent.

Move.

But the voice of self-preservation was smothered beneath the mounting yearning that had dogged her for three long weeks. Her willpower was eroded in the face of the need to experience what had happened in her suite just one more time.

Although would it stop at one? Or was she deluding herself?

'They are in the process of being retrained in other skills,' he replied to the question she had already forgotten. She told herself to focus.

'And after that?'

'Brilliant people like you will guide them towards the right jobs,' he stated simply.

A warm glow fired up inside her. 'So you do think I'm doing a good job?'

His gaze turned slightly mocking. 'Are you fishing for compliments, Esmeralda?'

'I'm seeking enlightenment as to why you grill me so hard every evening if you're happy with the job I'm doing.'

'Perhaps I give you a hard time because I don't want you to rest on your laurels. Or...' he drawled in an even deeper, lower voice, 'perhaps giving you a hard time is my way of coping.'

She stopped breathing altogether. 'Coping with what?' Her voice was just above a husky murmur.

'With the fact that I want you in my bed, beneath me, more than I want sustenance,' he admitted gruffly.

The warm glow erupted into an inferno, but a large dose of confusion remained. 'Then why haven't you done anything...or said anything before now?'

He gave an elegant roll of one shoulder that was more an animalistic stretch than a shrug. 'It was supposed to be a noble act. I wanted you to get embedded in your role without distractions. I was going to wait until we returned to my palace before making you mine.'

'But...?'

'But I find that there's only so much altruism I can stomach before I'm driven insane by the need to have you,' he growled.

Esme barely had time to brace herself against the wall of formidable man that came at her. Her scarf was tugged loose and disposed of, and the hair she'd pinned up minutes ago was freed within seconds, even as he bore her back against the cushions.

His large, muscular body covered hers, and his lips met hers in a hot, demanding kiss she felt all the way to her toes. She'd thought the first time they'd kissed that it couldn't get any better, that the need inside her couldn't get larger or hungrier.

But as her fingers tunnelled through his thick hair with urgency and greed, Esme was introduced to another level of need so great she actually whimpered with the thought of it going unsatisfied. Whether he sensed it or not, Zaid fed that need with renewed vigour, mouth and tongue and teeth ravaging hers in a relentless erotic dance that had her already dizzy senses spinning.

Strong muscled thighs parted hers, and he settled himself more firmly over her. As if he already owned the right to be there. Esme knew she'd given him that right, that with her silence these past three weeks she'd completely accepted that this was going to happen.

She would give her virginity to Sultan Zaid Al-Ameen.

A jet of alarm sprouted inside her, attempting to cool the blazing fires. She didn't need lessons in sex and sexuality to know twenty-five-year-old virgins were as rare as hen's teeth. But whereas the choice not to explore her sexuality had been solidly accepted and acceptable in her own mind, suddenly it occurred to her that it might not be the case from another's perspective.

The possibility of disappointing him suddenly loomed large in her mind, tossing another bucket of cold water over her frenzied senses.

The warm pads of his fingers drifted down her cheek, insisting on her attention and immediately receiving it. Brought back to the stunning desert oasis and the equally stunning, virile male whose eyes broadcast his ravenous hunger for her, she almost managed to convince herself her worries weren't warranted. A shaky sigh escaped her as he lowered his head, trailing kisses on her bottom lip and along her jaw. 'I'm attempting not to allow the fact that I've clearly lost your interest to dent my ego too much,' he drawled in her ear.

Short, shocked laughter barked out of her. To think he was remotely disturbed by the same worry that plagued her! 'Your ego has nothing to worry about from me.'

She sobered when he raised his head and she saw the speculative gleam swirling in his eyes. 'You want me,' he stated, a touch arrogantly, his hand leaving her cheek to chart a path of fire down her throat to the open neckline of her tunic.

She couldn't deny it, although the depth of it shocked her. 'Yes, I want you,' she gasped.

A rough inhalation expanded his chest as his lips continued to wreak havoc on her bare skin. 'Now we've got the most important detail out of the way, tell me the source of your second thoughts and I will deal with them.'

Esme bit her lip. Dared she risk telling him? Would he care? What if he stopped making love to her?

She held her breath as he raised his head again, the speculation much more intense this time. 'Esmeralda, what is it?' he demanded.

She slicked lips gone dry. 'I'm feeling a little bit out of my depth. I… I haven't done this before,' she stuttered.

He stared silently down at her for a full minute before he jumped lithely to his feet. The realisation that she'd lost him that quickly, that easily, stunned her so completely she stared mutely at him for endless seconds before she noticed the hand he was holding out to her. Warily, she placed her hand in his.

The moment she was upright, he swung her up into his arms. Esme's eyes widened.

'Zaid…'

He silenced her with a swift kiss before he strode out of the living room with long, purposeful strides. A short corridor later they walked through another opening and arrived in what could only be termed as the most masculine space she'd ever seen.

Animal-skin rugs graced the floor. Bold works of embroidered art hung on the walls. And in the middle of the floor a fire pit blazed with an intricate meshed metal dome that kept the flames contained.

But it was the bed that dominated her attention. Although it stood no higher than three feet off the floor, the emperor-sized bed, laid on exquisitely carved timber pallets, was enthralling in itself, even before the blinding-white satin sheets and the countless richly coloured pillows and cushions that graced the vast surface. Everything in the room screamed sensuality and endless luxury.

It also screamed that this place was reserved for those steeped in the art of lovemaking, and not for innocents such as herself.

The sensation of being out of her depth grew to stomach-churning proportions. She drew in another shaky breath as he lowered her to her feet.

Long, elegant fingers slid into her hair and angled her face up to his determined one. 'Your equivocation isn't unwarranted. This will be the first time I too will be mixing business with pleasure,' he confessed.

The drugging effect of his fingers on her scalp distracted her from his words for several moments. 'I... What?' she murmured faintly.

'That is what you're worried about, isn't it? That we risk compromising our professional relationship with a personal one?' he pressed, even as he stepped closer, brought his hips into singeing contact with hers and trailed his lips across hers once more. 'But the alternative is to deny ourselves this. And that, *habiba*, is not going to happen tonight,' he affirmed with deep, solid conviction.

Her mouth dropped open but coherent words failed to form. He thought she was reticent about sleeping with him because she was his employee!

The mouth hovering tantalisingly close returned to seal

over hers, his tongue breaching her lips with renewed sexual resolution that reinvigorated the fire inside her. With a helpless moan she clamped her hands around his shoulders, straining up to receive more of the drugging caress.

She needed to tell him. She *would* tell him. But not yet. After another kiss. Just in case all this came to an abrupt end the moment he found out she was so inexperienced.

They kissed until their breaths turned ragged, until touching over silk and satin was no longer enough. Until the need to feel skin on skin raged out of control. Somewhere along the line Zaid had shrugged off his robe. Her slippers had fallen off her feet, leaving her bare feet on soft rugs.

It was only when Zaid muttered urgently in Arabic against her lips that she started to heed the screaming voice in her head that told her she was running out of time to tell him. His hands were slowly drawing up her tunic, the soft breeze from a nearby opening sliding seductively over her skin.

She managed to free her tongue from the roof of her mouth. 'Zaid...'

'I need to see you,' he translated thickly. 'Touch you properly. Taste you.'

His hands brushed the side of her hips as he continued to tug up her dress, murmuring thick, sensual promises against her lips.

Her fingers convulsed against his sleek pectoral muscles as he worked to free her from the tunic. 'Zaid... I... have to tell you—'

'Shh, *jamila*, just give in to the pleasure.'

Before she could push the necessary words out, he was pulling the dress over her head. Her freed hair tumbled over her body in long tresses. He brushed the strands over her shoulders so he could better see her. Then he tossed away the tunic and stood looking at her with eyes that promised unforgettable, incandescent pleasure.

One hand lifted slowly, as if drawing out the pleasure, to trace her collarbone, causing her to gasp as desire arrowed hot and hard through her body.

'I knew you were beautiful but the reality far surpasses my imagination, *habiba*,' he said in a near growl as his fingers drifted over the lace that cupped her breasts.

'Zaid...'

'Stay,' he commanded gruffly, twin slashes of colour staining his haughty cheekbones as he dropped his hand and strolled lazily, imperiously around her body.

He stopped behind her, his breath catching audibly. A second later a quick tug released the clasp of her bra. He didn't free her completely from it but, despite her self-consciousness, Esme had never felt so desired, so aware of her body. Her own breath caught as one finger stroked her first vertebra, then followed the line down in a languid caress that had liquid heat pooling at her feminine core. He stopped just above the cleft of her buttocks, his touch lingering as he stepped closer to plant a kiss on one bare shoulder. Then the other. A moment later his fingers were hooking into the sides of her lace panties, tugging them over her hips. They dropped to the floor and she heard his guttural sound of appreciation.

Tell him. Tell him now before it's too late.

With equal amounts of dread and desire she spun on her heel to face him. The quick movement dislodged the loose bra. In the next instant the scrap of lace fell free from her body to join her panties, leaving her completely naked, bare to his avid gaze. He traced her from head to toe, lingering at the shadowed place between her legs.

'You are truly exquisite, Esmeralda,' he praised.

At the sight of the ferocious hunger etched on his face,

Esme almost gave up. But she'd made a promise never to lie or mislead.

'You...you misunderstood me when I said I hadn't done this before.'

It seemed to take a monumental effort for him to drag his gaze up from her tight-peaked breasts. A slow frown gathered on his dark brow. 'Then enlighten me, *habiba*, and do it quickly before my patience runs out,' he advised, his voice barely above a rough rumble.

'I mean that I'm...a virgin.'

He grew statue still, his eyes narrowing. Seconds ticked by, then his nostrils pinched on a sharp inhalation. 'That is impossible. You're twenty-five years old,' he said bluntly.

'I assure you it's not impossible. I've never slept with a man.'

Her statement seemed to trigger an emotion within him. One she breathlessly recognised as shockingly primal, stamped with a possessive fire that grew as he continued to stand there looking at her. But alongside that, as predicted, were questions that stormed through his eyes, even as his gaze rushed feverishly over her body.

She pre-empted them by placing a hand on his chest. 'It was my choice not to explore that side of my life.'

He nodded, but the speculation remained. 'And you choose to bestow such a gift on me now because...?'

It occurred to her that his power and position in life would have made him suspect such a gift. 'Not because of who you are, if that's what you're wondering. If I was that calculating I would've waited until...until you saw the evidence for yourself, not risked you rejecting me because you thought I was being untruthful. But... I want you, more than I want to keep my innocence. I told you because... I didn't want... I know my inexperience may be a turn-off for you—' She stopped, flushing as he made a gruff sound of disbelief.

He stepped closer, bringing his body heat, the very temptation of him into her personal space. 'You think what you've just told me makes you less desirable to me?' he demanded. He followed the statement with another singeing full-body appraisal.

Standing there, naked, while he was fully clothed and she was *dying* with need was suddenly too much. Her head dipped beneath the weight of her want, her arms rising to block the most private parts of her body from him.

He lunged forward, grabbing her hands as his breaths emerged in harsh pants. 'Don't hide yourself from me, *habiba*. I want to see you, all of you. I wish to commit every magnificent inch of the body that is about to become mine and mine alone to memory.'

Her breath caught, her head jerking up to meet his gaze. Pure fire blazed in the topaz depths, robbing her of words, of the fear of rejection she'd dreaded.

'I...' She would never know what she planned to say because the words shrivelled and died in her throat when he reached behind him and tugged his tunic off in one decisive move. His massive chest was a hairless, contoured landscape of honed muscles and bronze-skinned perfection. Her mouth dried up and the need to touch him flared wildly through her as he hurriedly toed off his loafers, then removed his trousers.

Zaid was by far the most superior male specimen she'd ever clapped eyes on. She reeled as her voracious gaze took in lean hips, powerful thighs and a body so magnificent she didn't think she could stand to look at him for much longer without screaming that he take her. But still she looked her fill, especially at the proud manhood, fully engorged and straining against his stomach. The thought of all that power directed at her, *inside* her, sent a wave of dizziness through her. But it was accompanied by an undeniable hunger.

As if he read her thoughts, he caught her hand, drew it to his body. 'Give in to your desire, Esmeralda. Touch me,' he ordered roughly.

She gladly gave in. And gasped in wonder and delight as her fingers met feverishly hot smooth skin layered over rock-hard muscle. A strong wish to circle his magnificent body, just as he'd done to her, assailed her. But she didn't think she could move from where she was rooted to the spot, such was the awesome power surging through her.

So she contented herself with learning the grooves of his abs, of skimming her fingers over his breastplate, grazing her nails over his flat nipples. At his harsh hiss, her fingers froze.

The next moment, he cupped her nape in a jerky movement, bringing her flush against his body before slamming his mouth on hers. The kiss was hard, and quick, and spoke of an edge riding him he was hanging onto with great difficulty.

Just as abruptly he ended the kiss and swept her into his arms.

'We need to move this to the bed, sweet one. Now. Before I reach the point of no return and take you here on the floor.'

CHAPTER TEN

THE TOUCH OF the cool sheets against her back sent a delicious shiver through Esme. That shiver turned into a warm shudder when Zaid's hot, virile body settled over hers. He didn't return to kissing her, but instead trailed his mouth over her cheeks, her forehead, the tip of her nose before journeying down her throat to the pulse that raced wildly there. Through it all, he murmured deep, lyrical words in his own language. She didn't care that she had no understanding of them, as they pulsed with meaning in her blood. Emotion that felt different from the physical magic happening to her tightened in her chest. She didn't have time to explore it because his lips were destroying her very sanity.

They deposited kisses between the valley of her breasts for an interminable age, before cresting her left breast to tug one tingling nipple into his mouth.

Just like last time, the sensation was beyond exquisite. Her fingers convulsed where they'd been trailing though his hair. 'Oh!'

Encouraged by her response, he repeated the caress, then graced her twin nipple with the same incredible attention. By the time he continued on his exploration, Esme was nearly incoherent with pleasure. So much so it took a moment to realise his next destination.

Her breath froze as he wrapped one hand around her slim thigh and parted her legs. Throughout her feverish imaginings of what making love with Zaid would feel like, she'd never factored in oral sex. The aggressive determination on his face, however, told her he'd very much factored it into his own process and was intent on fulfilling that wish.

Heat surged high and fiery beneath her skin as he bared her most intimate body part to his bold gaze. The hand that captured her thigh released her to caress a path of devastation up to her heated core. Sure fingers parted her, his gaze flickering up to meet hers for a charged second before dropping back down to her centre.

'You're beautiful, Esmeralda,' he stated throatily. Simple words. But their effect on her was nothing short of earth-shattering.

The last of her resolve melted away, leaving her with a bone-deep belief that whatever happened when the sun rose tomorrow, she was doing the right thing right now. As if he'd read her thoughts, his eyes met hers, the darker depths staying fixed on her face for a long spell before he lowered his head and tasted her in the most elemental of ways.

Newly freed from her self-doubt, she succumbed to the pleasure racing through her bloodstream. The warm satin sheets slid gloriously underneath her as she gave in to the instinct to roll her hips against Zaid's caress. He made a gravelly sound of approval in his throat. She moved again, meeting the expert flick of his tongue against the engorged nub that was the epicentre of her pleasure. Fireworks burst across her vision, and her breath emerged in harsh pants as an indescribable sensation began to take over. It gathered speed and power, catapulting her higher with each bold caress from Zaid. Her fingers clenched into the satin sheets as he spread her even wider, and deepened the intimate kiss.

The giant knot of pleasure burst wide open without warning, drawing a shocked scream from her lungs as she was flung high into a stratosphere of pure, incandescent bliss. The pleasure rolled in an endless loop, her body convulsing shamelessly as she drowned in it. When it finally released her from its vicious grip, her eyes fluttered open. To the sight of the man responsible for her incredible release.

His hands were clamped on her hip and in her hair, and the dark flush on his face spoke of his own savage need. The need to bestow on him a fraction of what he'd just given her urged her to raise a hand to his cheek, caress his taut skin, before raising her head to press her lips to his.

A pure animal sound ripped from his throat as he quickly donned a condom, levered his body over hers and resumed the kiss. His thighs parted hers and she felt the undeniable power of his arousal between her legs. She looked down at where they were about to join. Her heart caught, the reality of his impressive girth forcing an apprehensive swallow.

The fingers in her hair tightened a touch, directing her attention upward. 'It'll be all right, *habiba*. Don't fret. The pain will be fleeting... I've been told. Then I guarantee you untold pleasure.'

His promise settled her nerves, as did, astonishingly, his intimation that she was his first innocent. For some reason that knowledge made the already tight band of unrecognisable emotion in her chest tauten. She had no time to dwell on it, however. He was taking her mouth again, although this time the kiss was gentle. Or as gentle as a powerful man who rode the very edge of his control could be. One hand left her hair to retake control of her thigh.

'Esmeralda.' Her name was a hoarse command as he opened her even wider.

One she heeded by lifting her gaze to his. Eyes almost black with intense lust seared hers as the crown of his penis breached her core. Dizzy excitement warred with the unknown.

'Put your arms around me,' he ordered.

She obeyed. Her fingers slid around and latched onto the hot, smooth skin of his lower back.

Then, with a single, guttural oath, he pushed himself inside her.

The sharpest lance of pain arched through her, snatching a helpless scream from her throat. His mouth clamped on hers, devouring the sound as if it belonged to him. And right at that moment it did. They both stilled, breathing ragged, bodies clenched as they fought through pleasure and pain. The pain wasn't as fleeting as he'd said. It gripped her as if wanting her to remember this moment. To imprint on her psyche the awe and magnitude of sharing her body with Zaid Al-Ameen.

After a handful of heartbeats he lifted his head to look at her as he drew back and surged into her again.

Pain diminished, dissolved, then gave way to pleasure. A different, more potent pleasure than that she'd experienced a little while ago. On the third thrust, Zaid buried himself to the hilt inside her. They both groaned.

His thrusts gained pace, the strokes of possession masterful.

His hand left her thigh to clamp on her hip, holding her in place as he kept his promise to make her completely his. And through it all he watched her, his gaze intense as he absorbed every particle of her pleasure, fused it with his.

Her eyes rolled. Her fingers dug into his back. The scream that rose this time was one of awe and bliss she'd never dreamed possible.

'Zaid...' Her sigh of his name was meant to ground her in this room, on this plane of reality for a little while longer, but it was no use.

She was soaring once again, but this time towards a higher state of bliss she knew instinctively would change her for ever. His relentless pace told her he intended to make sure of it.

Sweat bathed her skin, bathed his as the intensity of their coupling grew to a breaking point. She clamped her legs around his waist in an instinctive move. One that pleased him enough to draw a hoarse moan from him. And then, between one moment and the next, she was caught in the grip of a wild, ecstatic fever.

'Zaid!'

'Yes,' he groaned above her. 'Give in to it. Take all of it.'

'Oh… God.' Surrender had never felt so right. Esme flew higher than before, but not before she felt him lower his head to whisper in her ear.

'*Habiba*.' Sweetheart. Darling. She'd heard many Ja'ahrians use that term of endearment. But coming from Zaid at that moment, Esme felt as if he'd showered her with a thousand priceless gems.

Tears prickled the back of her eyes, and finally, she let go completely.

Zaid couldn't tear his gaze from the beautiful woman writhing in ecstasy beneath him. Everything about her captivated him. It had from the first moment he'd seen her, but nothing had prepared him for this. For his total absorption in her pleasure or the reality that it triggered his own to an unconscionable level.

He never wanted it to end. Although he knew, like all things, that it would. It must. He didn't understand the part of him that already deeply mourned that future loss. Neither did he want to dwell on it right now. That would be a problem for when the sun rose.

For now…

Her back arched from the bed as bliss rolled over her. Presented with the perfection of her breasts, he lowered his head and fed his wild hunger. She felt exquisite. Her body was a magnificent prize he wanted to gorge on for a very long time.

As for the gift of her innocence she'd bestowed on him? The thrill of primitive pleasure that had stormed his blood at her confession had only intensified the moment he'd penetrated her. He hadn't needed the visual evidence he was sure was staining his sheets to know she'd spoken the truth. He'd felt it and revelled shamelessly in it.

She gave another cry beneath him, her nails scoring grooves in his back as her pleasure reached its zenith. He held out for as long as he could. Until, feeling the strong ripples of her flesh milking his own, he finally succumbed to the sublime ecstasy that beckoned.

The roar that ripped from his throat was as primal as the sexual act itself. Zaid wasn't ashamed to admit it was the most electric, intense climax he'd ever experienced. One that perhaps could be repeated, given that even as their bodies cooled in the aftermath, he was already anticipating their next coupling?

He gathered her close, exhaling in satisfaction when her hand stole up his body to rest on his chest. He smoothed her hair back from her face and pressed a kiss on her forehead. Watched her beautiful mouth curve in a tired post-coital smile and her stunning eyes begin to droop in slumber.

Reluctantly, he let her sleep because she needed to recover from her first sexual experience. And also because he wanted time to sift through the questions crowding his brain. Although one question that had gnawed at him had been answered.

Surely if she'd held onto her virginity in the hope of gaining the maximum prize for such a gift, she would have been better off staying in the high-rolling world her father favoured, where wealthy men paid a handsome price for such acquisitions, and not as a lowly social worker serving the less fortunate?

He didn't doubt that there was more to the estrangement between father and daughter than she let on, but in this Zaid was sure she was playing with a straight bat. It was the same honesty and integrity with which she'd gone about helping his people in the past weeks, many of whom she'd befriended in the process. According to Fawzi, Esmeralda Scott had gained, in such a short time, the respect and admiration of the people she'd met. Her daily reports had also shown an in-depth understanding of how to best serve each community. Zaid had known very quickly that he couldn't have picked a better candidate for the job of helping him to rebuild the Ja'ahrian communities his uncle had neglected so badly.

The only fly in the ointment was her father.

In the dimming firelight of his tent Zaid's jaw clenched. So far, her one weakness seemed to be Jeffrey Scott. Perhaps the sooner his fate was determined, the sooner she could focus properly on other matters.

Like on his kingdom? On him?

His arms tightened around her. Why not? The memorable interlude they'd shared in his bed would run its course eventually, as most things did. But there was no rational argument for that course not to be prolonged for as long as possible if they both wished it to. No reason at all.

So he would make that happen.

Satisfied, he pressed another kiss to her forehead, then let the blissful sleep that beckoned finally take him.

Even though the tent was still in darkness when she woke, Esme knew dawn was creeping very close. The coals in the fire pit no longer blazed high, although the room still held its sultry warmth. A cockerel's crow a moment later was accompanied by sounds of a rising camp.

She kept her eyes shut as memories of last night surged along with wave after wave of incredulity. She'd given her virginity to Zaid. The experience had been awe-inspiring both during, and afterwards, when she'd woken up more than once in the middle of the night to find his strong arms clamped around her as if he wouldn't let her go. Each time, she'd returned to sleep with her heart lifting with an emotion she was too scared to label.

That undefined emotion and the fact that she instinctively knew she was alone in bed right now kept her from opening her eyes just yet. Once she did, she'd have to face the day. Have to face the fact that she'd changed for ever.

So she listened to the camp sounds for a minute. Then, bracing herself, she opened her eyes. The confirmation that Zaid wasn't in the room made her stomach dip alarmingly. Esme firmed her lips and sat up in bed. She'd known this was a one-time thing. The quicker she learned to accept that fact the quicker she could get back to her assigned role in Zaid's life. Except that stern talking to brought nothing but a tightening in her chest and a yearning for that not to be the case.

Well, wishes weren't horses...

Determinedly, she pushed her tousled hair back from her face, and was looking around for her clothes when the tent flap to a previously unseen opening in the bedroom folded back to reveal the man dominating her thoughts.

Zaid was shirtless. His dark hair was ruffled as if fingers—her fingers—had tossed it into its sexily dishevelled state. Dark shadow graced his unshaven jaw, giving him a rakish look that sent a dozen sparks of renewed need firing through her belly. And the soft black pants that rode oh-so-low on his hips? She swallowed, unable to decide which part of the magnificent man to feast her eyes upon. Memories of all that power, all that majesty, devoted to her pleasure in the dark of night made her stomach flip in giddy excitement, despite the voice inside her head that screamed caution.

His steps slowed as his gaze fixed on her, his eyes growing a shade darker as his gaze roved over her body. Belatedly, she remembered she too was bare from the waist up. Self-consciously, she dragged the sheet up to cover her breasts.

His eyes narrowed a touch as he approached. 'Good morning, Esmeralda,' he rasped when he stopped beside the bed.

Suddenly tongue-tied, she dragged her gaze from his mouthwatering torso to his face. 'Um...hi.'

He moved as if to climb onto the bed, but then he froze. Her furtive glance showed his gaze fixed at a point on the bed. She followed his gaze, then blushed furiously at the sight of tell-tale stains on the white sheet.

Her hand dashed out, her intention to tuck the sheet away. He caught hold of her wrist, his grip implacable as his gaze returned to hers.

'No.' That was all he said. But he didn't need to say any more. The primitive look in his eyes, increased a hundred-fold from last night, said it all. He'd been her first and he wanted the evidence on full display. Had this been a thousand years ago, she was certain he would have roared and beaten his male chest in arrogant triumph.

For some absurd reason, considering the fiercely charged moment, she had the strongest urge to smile. An urge she couldn't quite prevent.

His eyes gleamed as he caught her expression. 'Something amusing you, *habiba*?'

She blushed. Inhaled shakily as the fingers that held her caressed the pulse racing at her wrist. 'You should see your face. You look...'

'Tell me,' he invited as she hesitated.

'You look like you've savaged a dozen predators in order to win some sort of grand prize,' she said with an embarrassed smile.

His expression grew even more charged, his gaze slowly lowering to the sheet and then back up to hers. He let go of her wrist, prowling onto the bed until he was poised over her like the fierce marauder she'd likened him to. The kiss he slanted over her mouth was the last word in shameless, dominant claiming. The power of it bore her back onto the bed, even as she parted her lips to take everything he had to give.

The claiming was long and thorough, her senses swimming by the time he lifted his head. Topaz-dark eyes gleamed ferociously at her.

'I look like this because I *have* won a grand prize. Make no mistake,' he assured her. 'One I intend to keep.'

Esme was floundering to grasp the meaning of the last part of his statement when he rose off the bed again, drew the sheet away from her body and scooped her up in his arms.

Face flaming anew, she wrapped her arms around his neck and buried her face in his throat. 'Where are we going?' she mumbled when he began to stride across the room.

'You'll see,' he replied.

A little alarmed, she turned her head just as he stepped through the tent flap.

The high walls were made of the same hardened leather used to construct some of the sandstorm-proof shelters around the camp. This one was over ten feet high, built around a private oasis garden, in the middle of which stood a natural spring pool surrounded by a profusion of exotic shrubs and flowers.

The breath-taking sight made Esme temporarily forget she was naked in Zaid's arms, her gasp at the natural beauty surrounding her echoing in the dawn-encroaching space around them. 'Oh, my God, this place is amazing!'

A hint of a smile touched his lips as he strolled towards the pool. 'I'm glad you like it. My security team insisted on the walls to guard my privacy. I didn't want it at the time, but I am glad of it now,' he murmured in her ear as he slowly lowered her to her feet.

He glided his fingers down her side to rest on her hips as he took her mouth in another searing kiss. By the time he raised his head their bodies were plastered together, their breathing ragged. The strong hands clamped on her hips moved to cup her behind, long enough for Esme to become bracingly aware of his potent arousal against her belly before he drew her away.

'Take off my pants, *habiba*,' he ordered huskily. The combination of the American accent he'd never quite lost and the lyrical Arabic of the endearment was so sexy she couldn't stop the decadent shiver that raced through her.

She slowly disentangled her arms from around his neck, drifting her fingers down his naked shoulders. Last night she'd been too overawed to linger in her exploration of him.

She still was, to be honest. But having been granted this chance she thought might never come again, Esme seized it with both hands. She drew her fingers over his collarbone, past the steady pulse that beat beneath taut bronze skin, over the solid beauty of his pecs. This time she lingered over the flat male nipples that hungrily puckered beneath her touch. She yearned to press her mouth to them, but she hesitated, her gaze flicking up to his.

His eyes were at a watchful half-mast, his breath held as he waited to see her next move.

Something in his eyes lent her a confidence she hadn't thought herself capable of. Or it could have been the re-lentless hunger that pounded through her bloodstream. Whatever. Esme lowered her head and flicked her tongue over the tiny nub as he'd done to her so many times dur-ing their lovemaking last night.

The hot hiss that issued from his lips made her freeze. About to straighten, she jerked in surprise when he speared his fingers through her hair and held her to her task. She repeated it. Revelled in the fierce tremble that shook his powerful frame. Overjoyed at his reaction, she kissed her way across his massive chest to the twin peak, all the while exploring the rest of his glorious body with her fingers.

He allowed her to explore for countless minutes, his breath growing louder and rougher as her fingers drifted lower, and her mouth and teeth left fiery trails on his skin.

When she reached the waistband of his pants, Esme took a quick, steadying breath, then slipped her hand beneath the soft material.

The power and might of him sent her temperature soaring. Steel wrapped in velvet. Majestic. Potent. Insanely intoxicating. She was so intent on familiarising herself with that part of his body she didn't hear his tortured groan until he grasped her hand and drew it away.

'How quickly you recognise and seize your power, *jamila*.' His voice was strained. Gravel rough. He kissed her palm, then dropped her hand back to his waistband with an autocratic quirk of his brow.

Reminded of her initial task, she took hold of his trousers and tugged them down, unable to stop the renewed rush of heat to her face when he stepped out of them and stood naked, proud and ready before her.

He was so beautiful he robbed her of breath.

The deeply magical moment continued as he led her down natural steps hewn into the rock of the pool. Cool and silky, the water submerged them to chest level before Zaid stopped. His fingers returned to spike through her hair, drawing her into his arms to kiss her one more time. After that he swam next to her before grabbing a sponge on a nearby surface. He washed her with slow, languid strokes, then washed himself with brisker movements. She read the intent in his eyes long before he tugged her decisively to the edge of the pool.

'I only meant for us to bathe in case you were sore after

last night, but I've been wanting to do this again for hours, Esmeralda,' he murmured, drawing her down on top of him as he sat on the lowest step.

'I'm fine,' she managed to gasp out.

Kisses peppered the corners of her mouth, her throat, before he ravenously latched onto her nipples. Hunger, deep and unstoppable, stung to life between her legs. Legs that he arranged on either side of his hips even while he continued to ravage her breasts. Heart racing, she braced her hands on his shoulders, anticipation making her rock forward in blind search of the pleasure only he could bring. Her feminine core found the head of his penis.

Abruptly, he tore his mouth from her nipples, his face a taut mask of untamed need. With one hand he grasped himself, the other bracing her as he surged upward, seating himself inside her in one powerful thrust.

Her gasp mingled with his groan. Their lips fused for one charged second before they separated again, returning to stare at each other as if their union needed the connection of their gazes. Breathless, silent, he withdrew and powered back inside.

Her mouth parted on another soundless gasp. She met him halfway on the third thrust, earning her a grunt of approval that ramped up the pleasure stealing through her bloodstream.

Eyes still fused to hers, he nodded. 'Yes, that's it.'

Movement as old as time dictated the roll of her hips as she rose for a moment, then drove back down. The sensation of power and control and pleasure mingled in a heady potion, driving her to seek more and more of it.

As the water splashed around them, Zaid's hands left her to spread long arms on the rim of the pool, his head going back as he lounged, imperiously like the master and commander he was, against the rock. Then half-closed eyes the colour of polished topaz watched her with heated encouragement as she propelled them both to the edge of the glorious abyss.

Something in his expression drove her to take him deeper, increase the pace of her movements. His face grew tauter, twin swathes of colour staining his cheekbones as his breathing turned choppier. 'Yes,' he encouraged hoarsely. 'Take me, *habiba*, as I have taken you.'

Esme didn't need a second bidding. Fingers splaying on either side of his strong neck, she gave in to the siren song whispering through her body.

It wasn't long before the crescendo built to insane proportions, and Zaid's groans were turning guttural. Feeling even bolder than before, she stole another kiss from his sensual lips, then got lost in it when he took over. Connected in every possible way, they tumbled over the edge in unison, devouring each other's vocal expression of the nirvana they were drowning in.

They were still connected when his strong arms came around her and he rose from the pool and strode, dripping wet and not caring, back into the tent.

They were still fully connected when he lowered her onto the bed and then he froze for a split second, his eyes going wide with shock, before he disengaged and flung himself away from her with an ear-bleeding curse.

CHAPTER ELEVEN

SHE DIDN'T NEED a cipher to know something was wrong. Very wrong.

'Z-Zaid?' Hard on the heels of her earth-shattering climax, her voice was nowhere near steady as she watched him pace from one end of the tent to the other. For a mad instant she was jealous of his ability to do so while unashamedly naked. In contrast, Esme couldn't pull the sheet—the newly changed sheet, she absently observed—over her body fast enough.

'I cannot believe—' He stopped, went a little white, then turned his back on her one more time. He completed two more lengths of the room before he stopped at the foot of the bed, out of touching distance. 'We didn't use any protection just now...in the pool,' he stated in a grave voice steeped in dark regret.

She went cold despite her taking another few moments to fully grasp his meaning. When she did, her stomach hollowed out. Then, forcing herself to think, she blurted, 'I'm...on the Pill.'

The immense relief that crossed his face was almost comical. Almost. Because something severed any trace of laughter from her heart before she had time to absorb it.

And also because a frown was beginning to replace that relief. 'Why were you on the Pill if you weren't sexually active?' he whipped at her.

'Because my doctor recommended it to help regulate my periods,' she explained.

He exhaled. Nodded as relief returned, full blown. His fists started to unclench.

Just as memory began to poke holes in her hasty assurance.

He started to round the bed towards her. Then he froze again when he saw what must have been near horror on her face.

'But... I...'

'But what, Esmeralda?' he snapped.

'I ran out last week, when we were in Dishnaja. Nashwa managed to get a prescription filled for me yesterday, but I missed three doses...' Her voice trailed off as the enormity of the consequences hit her. Had she been standing, she was certain she would have lost the use of her legs. As it was, she felt the blood drain out of her head at the grim look that overcame Zaid's features.

'Three doses, so three days' worth?' he pressed, his face once again rigid with tension.

She nodded miserably.

'What are the repercussions of missing them?'

Dread steeped deeper. 'Anything more than one missed dose and... I have to use extra precautions,' she whispered raggedly.

He uttered another curse in his language, then sank heavily on the mattress. Still out of reach. Ominous silence ensued.

'Zaid, I didn't think...when you summoned me here last night, this...what happened wasn't what I was expecting.'

He rubbed a hard hand over his jaw. 'That is inconsequential in the circumstances. Once is all it takes. And if there is blame to be laid, I'm far more culpable in this than you. It was my responsibility, and while I have no excuse for my carelessness, I will say in my defence that you enchanted me to a degree that I forgot myself.'

At any other time, his words would have filled her heart with joy. Not now, though. Not when they were delivered in a clipped tone that told her he was berating himself a thousand different ways for the situation they now found themselves in.

'When will you know?' he asked after another sharp exhalation.

She made a quick calculation. 'I'm not expecting my period for another two weeks, but I can take an early pregnancy test in about nine or ten days' time. Or I can...the morning-after pill is an option if that's what you want—'

'No! It is not. You will not get rid of my child before we even know there is a possibility of one.'

A wave of relief hit her at his vehement rejection of the remedy that had disturbed her to even consider, despite reeling at the possibility that she might be pregnant. Last night had been monumental. But it was nothing compared to the realisation that there could be long-lasting consequences to what they'd done.

'Zaid... I don't know if I can—'

Strong hands seized her shoulders, cutting her off. But, unlike last time, there was no tenderness in his face, no promise of untold pleasure blazing from his eyes. 'Don't say it. Don't even think of uttering words that would deny my child's existence.'

'I wasn't. But I'm not prepared for any of this.'

Lips she'd kissed barely half an hour ago flattened before he sighed and released her. She sagged back into the bed as he trailed his fingers down her arm to capture her hand. But again there was no hint of warmth, and it felt more like a way of making sure she stayed where she was. In case she what? Bolted? Esme was sure her legs wouldn't carry her one single step, never mind to anywhere far enough away from this tent to give her some peace of mind.

'We will step back from the edge of any hasty decision. We will get dressed and start the day with something as mundane as breakfast.'

She contained the urge to break into hysterical laughter. Nothing about the everyday life of Zaid Al-Ameen would ever be considered mundane, even the food he ate. 'And then what?'

'Then we will consider our options. Ones that *don't* include taking drastic measures. Are we agreed?' The question was filled with purpose.

And because she needed time too to absorb everything that had happened since she'd followed Fawzi into this tent last night, she answered, 'Yes, we're agreed.'

And just like that the subject was shelved. He let go of her hand and rose from the bed, then left the room without a backward glance.

When she was sure her legs would keep her upright, Esme stood and dressed in the clothes from the night before, which had been folded and placed on the chair at the bottom of the bed. Then, unsure of whether to leave or wait for Zaid, she dawdled for another half an hour in the bedroom.

Eventually, it was one of the servants who came in and beckoned her out to where Zaid was already seated on floor cushions spread around the dining area.

Breakfast was a feast of fruit, nuts, yoghurt, pastries, an assortment of juices, tea and coffee, served in respectful silence by a clutch of servants who bowed and smiled at their noble ruler, and cast keenly speculative glances her way. If the notion lingered for a moment that the women's interest in her this morning was far greater than it had been yesterday, or the day before, Esme had no room to dwell on it. Not when the subject of a baby... Zaid's baby...had taken over every corner of her mind.

She declined all but a piece of tangerine, a slice of toast and a small helping of honeyed yoghurt. Although Zaid's lips firmed, he didn't comment, his brow clamped as he remained deep in his own thoughts.

The moment the meal was cleared away, she stood to retrieve her scarf in anticipation of returning to her own tent. Absently she noted that it too had been moved and neatly folded on a low armoire in the living room. About to pick it up, she froze.

Zaid might be the Sultan, but his life wasn't his own. It never would be. It was a life he'd been destined for from the moment of his birth, a life he'd been trained for and embraced even while he'd been exiled.

Whereas she...

Esme swallowed. On the wild chance that she'd fallen pregnant, her life, or at least a huge part of it as the mother of the future heir of Ja'ahr, would be lived in this same, exotic fishbowl, no matter where on earth she chose to reside. She would be scrutinised at every turn. And as the daughter of Jeffrey Scott, her past too would become a source of interest.

Her past would be exposed. Including her role in her father's life before she'd walked away from him. And what had happened in Vegas. With Bryan.

Her outstretched hand trembled so badly she clenched it into a fist.

'What's wrong?' Zaid demanded sharply.

She jumped and spun around to face him. Intelligent eyes were locked on her, examining her every breath, her every blink. The all-black traditional attire he'd changed into gave him an air of a merciless conqueror, despite the white trim bordering the material. 'I... I'm afraid shelving this isn't as easy as I thought it would be. Yesterday I was just a social worker, assigned to do a job I know and love. Today I'm...'

'You're the Sultan's lover, and the woman who could be carrying the next heir of Ja'ahr,' he intoned baldly, leaving no room for equivocation.

The tremble in her hand transmitted to her whole body.

For a single moment Esme found herself praying that his seed had not taken root inside her. If for no other reason than because of the shame she would bring on her child, its father, and the people of Ja'ahr should her secret be discovered. She clenched her gut against the guilt and pain that followed on the heels of that thought.

'Esmeralda?' His autocratic voice brought her mind back into focus.

She turned and snatched up her scarf. 'I'm going back to my tent. I expect you have…um…people waiting to meet with you.'

His frown intensified, but after a moment he nodded. 'I'll ensure you're not disturbed while you rest.'

Esme had very little doubt she would be doing any resting but, eager to escape his probing scrutiny, she nodded and murmured her thanks.

She passed Fawzi, who bowed suspiciously deeply the moment he spotted her. Walking through the camp, Esme also began to notice the marked difference in the greetings that came her way. Where they'd been open, carefree before, their greetings were now accompanied by respectful bows and almost deferential smiles.

They knew she'd spent the night in Zaid's bed. They probably knew she'd been sexually innocent. And now they were attempting to place her on a pedestal on which she didn't belong. The guilt congealing inside her had grown into an unbearable stone by the time she stumbled into her tent.

About to give in to the sobs that bubbled in her throat, she forced them back down when Aisha and Nashwa rushed in after her.

'His Highness says that you are to rest,' the older woman said. 'Aisha will make you some jasmine tea to—'

'No tea, thank you, Nashwa,' she said firmly. 'I just want to lie down for a bit, if that's okay.'

'Of course, Madam.'

She glided past her, heading for the bedroom, while Aisha stepped up and gently tugged the scarf from her hand. Aware that the women wouldn't rest until they felt they'd been of service, Esme succumbed to being attended to, then sighed in relief the moment they retreated.

But the relief didn't last against the thoughts tearing her mind apart. Her secret wasn't the kind she could keep to herself, but it also wasn't the kind she would wish for Zaid to be blindsided by. And then there was the inescapable truth that publicly admitting what she knew about her father's past would hammer another, possibly irredeemable, nail in his coffin.

She grabbed the nearest pillow and buried her face in it. But as much as her head wanted to wind the clock back to this time yesterday, where the extent of her problems was whether Zaid wanted her or not, her heart wouldn't allow that wish to remain. Because then she wouldn't have experienced the most magical hours of her life. And if there was a baby growing inside her... Her breath caught.

She had a little time before she found out one way or the other. Maybe, Zaid too, with time to think, wouldn't feel so strongly about claiming a child whose mother was a nobody and whose grandfather was a criminal. For all she knew, he might prefer her and her child to exist far away from his kingdom. Then all she would have to worry about was how to protect her baby from the shaky legacy of her past.

The effort it took to block out the mocking voice that ridiculed her thinking that Zaid wouldn't claim her child finally wore her out. She was staring blankly at the wall of the tent when she heard excited voices, followed by the unmistakeable sound of rotors approaching.

A glance at her phone showed she'd been lying in bed for two hours. Although she wasn't due to meet with the teachers of the community for another hour, Esme rose, slid off the tunic and went into the bathroom to splash water on her face. She changed into another tunic, this one in a deep blue. She added the accompanying accessories and walked out into the living room, just as Zaid walked in.

His eyes raked her from head to toe, his face unsmiling. 'You're dressed to travel. Very good.'

'Why? Are we going somewhere?' she asked.

'Yes, we're retuning to the Royal Palace.'

She frowned. 'But we still have a day's work to finish here. I'm meeting the teachers in an hour.'

'The report you drew up yesterday was more than sufficient. Any further assessments can be done by other means.'

'What other means?'

He gestured impatiently. 'Phone calls. Video conferences. A dozen other different ways. We're not a backwater tribe, you know.'

'Of course I know. I wasn't suggesting that at all.'

'Then let's go,' he commanded, holding out his hand in imperious emphasis when she hesitated.

'Why do I feel that there's more going on here than you're telling me?'

A muscle rippled in his jaw. 'Because there is. I suggested that we take some time to absorb the possibility that you may be carrying my child. I was wrong to do so. If you are truly carrying my child—'

'A fact that is *still* only a possibility...

'Then we need to put certain arrangements in place,' he finished as if she hadn't spoken.

'What kinds of arrangements?' she demanded.

'The kind that you will be apprised of in due course.'

'So I will be the last one to know?'

'No, you will be one of the first to know when final decisions have been made.'

She wasn't going to get any more out of him. She knew it from the way he angled his body determinedly towards the door and expected her to fall in line. She knew it from the way Fawzi guided her towards the helicopter the moment she stepped out while Zaid said his goodbyes to the Tujullah elders. She knew it when he took his seat beside her and immediately activated his satellite phone.

As they soared into the air and the pilot pointed the aircraft towards the capital, Esme became blindingly aware of one thing. Whether her pregnancy had been confirmed or not didn't matter to Zaid. While his heir was even a possibility, he was going all out to lay his claim on it.

Zaid observed his small council of advisors as the monthly meeting came to an end. He knew the last un-itemised point of the meeting was about to be brought up because it had been broached, sometimes subtly, sometimes boldly, at each meeting for the last six months.

This time, though, he wasn't as disinterested by or dismissive of the subject as he'd been on previous occasions. In fact, there was a hum of anticipation within him that had been present ever since he'd walked into the room.

It had been ten days since he'd returned to the Royal Palace with Esmeralda. Ten days during which he'd tried to get to grips with the possibility that he might be a father. He hadn't sought confirmation yet, since his initial research had advised that it might still be too early. But, like he'd told Esmeralda, decisions needed to be made. And the more he'd weighed up all his options, the more he'd realised he had only one. More than that, though, was the realisation he couldn't keep avoiding the decision he'd been putting off. Whether Esmeralda was pregnant or not, he would have to marry some time in the near future.

He couldn't deny that marriage to a woman from an allied kingdom would bring another layer of stability to

Ja'ahr. But marriage and the announcement of an heir would be even more welcomed by his people.

Either way, it was a decision that needed to be addressed. So why not now?

And why not Esmeralda and the possible child she might be carrying?

Two birds...one stone...

He tented his fingers and focused on the oldest member of his group of advisors, an ageing man in his seventies who'd been a good friend and aide to his own father. Zaid trusted him because, aside from the sound counsel he'd given him, Anwar Hanuf was also the man who'd risked his life to save him the night his parents had been assassinated.

Anwar cleared his throat, and the room fell silent. 'At the risk of repeating myself for the umpteenth time, I think it's time you solidified your position as Sultan and married, Zaid.'

Zaid kept silent, an action that surprised Anwar since this was usually the time Zaid waved him away, stood up and brought the meeting to an abrupt end.

Anwar, seeing his opportunity, ploughed ahead. 'Our neighbouring states are dying to form firmer alliances through commerce, but one or two are also hoping for a much stronger alliance through marriage.' He stopped, and eyed Zaid. When Zaid nodded for him to continue, he hastily opened a dossier and reeled off a list of possible candidates.

Zaid shook his head after the fourth one. 'No. As much as I accept that arranged marriages forged in the name of stronger alliances have a good success rate among our people, that isn't going to work for me. I won't marry a woman I don't know, neither do I have the time to date and get to know one well enough to propose. But I do accept your argument that marriage will help stabilise our country.'

Anwar sat up straighter, keen black eyes probing Zaid. 'Do you also accept that it needs to happen sooner rather than later?'

'Yes. And I may already have a candidate,' he supplied.

The group exchanged glances. Anwar voiced the question blazing through their minds. 'The English woman?' he asked, a little deflated.

Zaid's eyes narrowed. 'Do you have a problem with her?'

'Of course not. Her suitability isn't the issue. But we are concerned about her father, your potential father-in-law.'

Zaid's jaw tightened. 'His fate lies with a jury of his peers, not with me. Whatever the verdict, we will deal with it.'

The men fell silent, absorbing his resolute reply. Anwar cleared his throat. 'There's concern that our enemies might use her father's situation to stir up trouble.'

He stiffened, recalling his conversation with the chief of police. 'Then they will be dealt with the same way we deal with criminals—using the letter of the law.'

Anwar nodded. 'Very well, Your Highness. We look forward to your instruction on when we can make a formal announcement.'

Zaid remained in the room after the men had departed. Had he jumped the gun a little where Esmeralda was concerned?

No.

Whether she was pregnant or not, his argument for marriage was a sound one. They were compatible both in bed and out of it. She'd proved in a short time that she could be very good for his people, her ability to adapt to his country and it customs stunningly impressive.

She was intelligent enough to know what was at stake. He was confident she would see that saying no to him wasn't an option.

* * *

'No.'

For the first time since she'd known him, Zaid looked lost for words. So was she, to be honest, since the last question she'd expected to hear from his lips were the ones he'd uttered a minute ago.

'Marry me?'

But the answer that powered from her soul stemmed from the knowledge that, even though her heart had leapt for a single moment, this was wrong. Perhaps it had also stemmed from the fact that the previous time she'd received a proposal, it had also been the under wrong circumstances. Plus she'd spent the last ten days in near isolation, Zaid's terse words that she remain in the palace when they'd returned from Tujullah ringing in her ears. He'd offered very little explanation save to say she'd earned a break after throwing herself into her work for three weeks. But she'd known there was more to the command.

Marry me.

The words weren't delivered with flowery sentiment or devotion, but with the gravity of a thousand drums behind them. Wherever he'd been these last few days, this conclusion had been well thought out and finalised. Without her input or approval.

'What did you say?' he finally demanded.

'I said no. I won't marry you. And before you narrow your eyes at me, we both know this proposal is based solely on the possibility that I might be pregnant.'

His eyes did narrow. And his body tensed too as he strolled to where she'd been admiring the garden in one of the many private courtyards that peppered the palace. She'd had a lot of time on her hands to explore over the past ten days. Each new discovery had been more breathtaking than the last. Esme didn't know whether she loved the Royal Palace more because she'd discovered that Zaid's parents had chosen to live in a hotel for three years while they'd built this palace from the ground up after they'd donated their old palace to an orphanage in desperate need of housing, or because each stone contained a rich history that spoke of the love and devotion Ja'ahrians held for Zaid's parents.

The knowledge that she was falling in love with the culture and people of Ja'ahr had crept up on her. The knowledge that she'd roamed the palace secretly, looking out for its ruler and wishing they were still out on the road when he'd been more accessible was a more disturbing discovery.

Her leaping senses absorbed his face, his voice, now even as she accepted that what he was asking of her was impossible.

'Of course it is,' he confirmed, his expression puzzled at her response. 'It's the right thing to do to legitimise my heir.'

Esme almost laughed. Only the peculiar ache lodged in her chest kept the sound from escaping. 'And how would waiting a few more days make a difference?' she asked, even though she knew marriage would be an impossible choice for her then, too. 'Or, better still, we can clear this up right now if you'll allow me to take an early pregnancy test.'

His frown deepened. 'Why are you convinced you're not carrying my child?'

'I'm not convinced. It's just I don't understand why you're waiting to find out. And I don't understand why you're proposing marriage. Like you said, your people are forward-thinking. Will they really question the legitimacy of your baby, *if* there is one, based on when exactly he or she is born?'

His jaw clenched. 'The general advice is to wait until two weeks have passed or better still once the date of your next cycle is exceeded to be definite. As for the timing of the marriage, I don't care what other people think. *I* would prefer that we move as quickly as possible. A wedding, especially one to a sovereign, takes time to plan and execute.'

She shook her head. 'But that's not everything, is it? What aren't you telling me, Zaid?'

He kept silent for so long she thought he wouldn't respond. He paced to the edge of the bubbling fountain, looking at it for a long moment.

'There's been a push for me to marry for a while now. A push I've resisted even though it's my destiny and duty to marry and produce heirs. But the time has come and I don't wish to wait any longer.'

Esme conjured up an image of a future Zaid, married to a faceless woman, one who would happily wear his ring and bear his children. The certainty it wouldn't be her sent a large dose of disquiet ringing through her, escalating her fear that her growing attachment to all things Ja'ahr extended to its ruler too.

Sternly, she pushed the suggestion away. She had too much baggage to ever contemplate such a thing.

'All the better reason for you to rule out a pregnancy quickly. Then once we discover that I'm not pregnant, you can find someone more appropriate to marry.'

He whirled to face her. *'Appropriate?'*

The laughter that finally emerged scraped her throat. 'Come on, Zaid. Would you have even considered me as a suitable bride had we not had a mishap with contraception?'

He had the grace to hesitate, to not insult them both by rushing to deny what she'd said. His lids veiled his expression for a moment before he looked back up at her. 'We are where we are. The only way is to be pragmatic about our situation.'

'This is absurd. An early pregnancy test will clear all

of this up. They're very reliable now. Then we can both go back to living our lives.'

For some reason that made his expression darker. 'You say that as if it's a separate thing. Have you forgotten that you've committed to living under my roof, under my protection, for as long as I require?' he asked.

'I haven't forgotten. But neither have I forgotten that it won't be for ever.' Again that punch of disquiet unnerved her at the thought of her future departure from Ja'ahr. From Zaid.

The observation displeased him even more. He stared at her for an age, before he reached out and caught her wrist in a firm hold, then began to lead her out of the courtyard. 'Very well, let's get this over and done with,' he rasped.

'Where are we going?' Esme demanded as she hurried to keep up with his longer strides.

'You're not prepared to wait another few days for a more accurate confirmation so we'll try things your way. But I'm agreeing on the basis that we will follow it up with more precise blood tests when the time comes.'

She'd had time to grow more familiar with the intricate layout of the Royal Palace in the last week and a half, so within a minute she knew they were headed for Zaid's private chambers.

'We're going to do the pregnancy test now?' she blurted, suddenly unsure whether she was prepared for it. Whether she was prepared for her future, her possible departure, to be made finite.

He slanted her a narrow-eyed look. 'Isn't that what you've been angling for?'

'But we... I don't have any kits.' She'd been unwilling to ask Nashwa to buy any for her because she hadn't wanted the speculation she knew was brewing to overflow.

She watched Zaid calmly extract his phone and hit dial.

After a few terse words were exchanged he hung up. 'Problem solved.'

She'd got what she wanted. And yet apprehension clawed up her spine the closer they got to his private wing. In minutes she'd know if her fate would be sealed with Zaid's for ever, or whether the clock would be starting a wind-down of her time in his life.

Esme wasn't surprised to see Fawzi waiting inside Zaid's lush, private living room with a rectangular box that looked like it had been dug straight out of Aladdin's treasure chest. With a deep bow and a cryptic look at her he handed the box over and left the room.

Zaid released her, then lifted the lid of the box. Inside, on a bed of red velvet, lay two early pregnancy test kits still sealed in their containers. He picked them up and held them out to her.

Her breath stalled in her lungs. The moment of truth.

Her fingers trembled as she took the items from him. A look at his face showed he too was in the throes of a deep, earth-shattering emotion. He set the box down and silently walked her through a set of white double doors that led to a bathroom.

The space was as jaw dropping as the rest of the palace, if not even more so. But all Esme could concentrate on was the fate that awaited her minutes from now.

And fate rammed home, loud and terrifying, in two sets of thick blue lines.

She had no recollection of walking back to the bathroom doors or opening them. Only of Zaid, tall and proud, breath held and immovable before her.

Waiting for the words she couldn't keep inside any more. 'I'm pregnant.'

CHAPTER TWELVE

SHE DIDN'T RECALL much of the moments following her announcement. It was as if those two words, once uttered, had expanded to fill every atom of her life. But, somehow, between one moment and the next, she was lying on a long velvet sofa with a grim, slightly pale Zaid crouched over her.

'What…what happened?' she ventured.

Eyes turned a dark bronze pierced almost accusingly into her. 'It seems I was wrong in thinking rationality would prevail once you had your answer. Instead, the knowledge that you're pregnant with my child seems to have adversely overcome you. You delivered the news and then promptly collapsed,' he stated sombrely.

Esme felt the room sway as the reality of it kicked her hard. She was pregnant. With Zaid's child.

Oh, God.

She shut her eyes. Took a shallow breath, then another when the first didn't quite make it to her lungs. When that didn't work, she gulped some more.

'It would please me greatly if you would stop hyperventilating.'

Because it wasn't good for the baby? She forced herself to take the next breath more slowly.

'Open your eyes, Esmeralda. We need to face this together,' he instructed heavily.

She obeyed only because he was right, no matter how much she wanted to slip into oblivion. He looked graver than before. 'Zaid…' Her voice was a choked noise that sounded worse lying down. She started to sit, only to find herself being pressed firmly back.

'Don't get up. The doctor is on his way.'

She started. 'What? I don't need a doctor!'

'That's a matter of opinion. Unfortunately for you, faint-ing into my arms takes the decision out of your hands.'

She sagged against the plump cushions, unwilling to ac-knowledge the weakness dredging through her at the feel of his hand through the thin cotton of her yellow sundress. In the next moment she realised his hand was splayed di-rectly over their baby. Her heart jumped as she watched the same thought occur to him.

His eyelashes swept down to veil his gaze. Esme didn't know whether to rejoice or mourn when he removed his hand a moment later.

He crossed to a nearby drinks cabinet and returned with a glass of water and a conveniently placed straw. She took a few sips under his intense scrutiny before he set the glass down.

Esme cleared her throat and tried again. 'I think you were right. We need to wait for the proper time to do the test again. Maybe this was a false positive...' She trailed off when a bleak, shuttered look entered his eyes.

'Does it fill you with that much horror, the idea of car-rying my child?'

Shock froze the blood in her veins. *'What?'*

'First you wanted to take the test immediately, but now we have the results, you want to deny the truth? A more paranoid man would think the idea of marrying me, of hav-ing my child, is abhorrent to you, *habiba*,' he said chill-ingly.

A single shake of her head was all she could manage in denial. 'No. You misunderstand. It's not you.' She stopped and took a breath, struggling to calm her racing mind. 'I just... I don't want you to make a mistake you'll regret,' she finished weakly.

Her explanation tugged a mirthless smile from him.

'You seem bent on saving me from myself. Do you think I didn't weigh all the options before arriving at my decision?'

How could he have, when he didn't have the whole truth?

Tell him!

'No, I don't think you have.'

'Then enlighten me.'

'I have too much baggage, Zaid. My father—'

One autocratic hand slashed through the air. 'You're nothing like your father,' he dismissed. 'If you were, I wouldn't have given you the position you hold. My people are already beginning to embrace you. My council of advisors has approved you as my bride. And for those still swayed by that sort of thing, it's already known that you were an innocent when I took you to my bed.'

The sharp left turn in the conversation jumbled her thoughts. 'What? How would they have...? Oh, the *sheets*?'

He shrugged, not in the least bit embarrassed by referring to a subject that made her face flame. 'The hard-core traditionalists will just have to be content with the wedding night coming after the deed.'

'Oh, my God,' she murmured incredulously, her head still spinning. A swipe of her tongue over lips turned dry, and she attempted again. 'Zaid, listen to me—'

'My grandmother was a second wife, did you know that?' he cut across her again. Was he doing it deliberately to stop her from telling him what she needed to?

'Um...no, I didn't know.'

'My grandfather's first wife was an American,' he continued. 'She was fully accepted, even loved by the people until her unfortunate, premature death. So, you see, Ja'ahrians aren't complete traditionalists when it comes to the wives their rulers take.'

'But there are other factions that won't welcome this,

aren't there?' she countered. 'Like whoever was pushing the chief of police's buttons?'

His jaw flexed. 'If he and they need reminding, I will merely reconfirm what I said to him the night I came for you.'

'Which was?'

'That you belong to me and I have taken you under my protection.'

Despite the foolish weakness threatening to overcome common sense, she grimaced. 'You make me sound like a chattel.'

'*He* was the one who intended to use you as a pawn. I needed to communicate with him in a language that he understood. I believe the message got through to him. If that's all you're worried about, rest easy.'

'It's not—' She was interrupted for the third time, but this time by a firm knock on the door. At Zaid's command, Fawzi entered with a tall, lean man with rimless glasses, greying hair and a brisk air of confidence.

After a hurried exchange of greetings, Fawzi departed, and the man approached her. 'I'm Dr Aziz. I understand you fainted?' The question was posed in a distinct American accent.

Surprised to hear it, she glanced at Zaid.

'Dr Aziz has been my personal doctor since I was a boy. He left Ja'ahr with me and I brought him back from the States when I returned. I trust him implicitly.' Simple words, but delivered with a thread of emotion that spoke of a bond between the two men.

The doctor cracked a smile as he opened his case. 'He means he trusts me not to tell you he's not as invincible as he likes everyone to think.'

His easy charm drew a smile from her. And a deep scowl from Zaid. 'Perhaps you would like to get on with seeing to your patient?'

'I'm fine, really—'

'She's pregnant.' Zaid calmly dropped the bombshell.

Dr Aziz hid his shock well as he looked from her to Zaid. 'This is great news, son. Congratulations.'

'Offer felicitations *after* examining her, Joseph,' Zaid clipped out.

The other man nodded. 'How far along are you?' he asked.

'I'm...um...we just did the tests,' Esme said.

'The relevant date you require is ten days ago,' Zaid added, naming the exact date.

Joseph Aziz frowned. 'It's too soon to be feeling faint.'

'Stop stating the obvious and fix her.'

'Zaid!'

The doctor smiled. 'Don't worry, I'm used to it. He gets cranky when he's worried.'

Zaid swung away, muttering under his breath. Joseph carried on unperturbed, asking her questions and taking notes on his tablet. He frowned again as she guiltily confessed to her recent loss of appetite. Five minutes later, he snapped his case shut.

'Well?' Zaid had returned, looming over them like a dark cloud.

'Nothing serious. Miss Scott is a little low on blood sugar. I'm guessing that, coupled with the momentous news that she's carrying our next Sultan, would throw anyone. She just needs to avoid skipping meals, and she'll be fine.' He offered her a reassuring smile, while Zaid stared at her with narrowed eyes as she finally sat up.

'I told you I was fine.'

'You and I have different definitions of fine, *habiba*, especially when you're not eating,' he rasped, before turning to Joseph. They exchanged a few words in Arabic before the doctor departed. And Fawzi re-entered moments later.

'Your Highness, your conference call is about to begin.'

Zaid nodded curtly and his assistant moved to a respectful but expectant distance. Her heart dipped.

'Zaid, we need to talk,' she murmured.

He faced her. 'You're carrying my child, Esmeralda,' he whispered fiercely. 'Nothing you have to say will shift the importance of that fact and our need to focus on it and it alone. From the moment you walked out of the bathroom, your arguments have become null and void.'

Her insides trembled as she shook her head. 'But you don't know—'

'Don't I? You're about to confess a less than stellar past association with your father.' He barely blinked as she gasped. 'But you forget that I know the sort of man he is. He's a gifted con artist in whose web you were caught at a vulnerable age.'

'There's more, Zaid,' she insisted.

He stepped close, clasped her shoulders. 'There's always more. But what matters is that you wised up and walked away eventually. The estrangement was your doing, was it not?' he pressed.

Lips pursed, she nodded. 'Yes.'

A hint of a genuine smile cracked his lips, before his face grew serious again. 'So you turned your life around. I don't need any more proof that my decision is sound.'

The sensation of sinking further into quicksand, despite the rope he was throwing her, escalated. 'Please, Zaid. Hear me out.'

'Your Highness?' Fawzi prompted.

Zaid sighed. 'You will marry me, Esmeralda. For the sake of our child you will marry me and we will make this work.'

A spurt of frustrated anger rose. 'Just like that?'

The fierce eyes that raked her face held a banked hunger that turned her anger into something equally primal. 'Trust me, *jamila*, nothing that happens between us will

ever be *just like that*. But for now you'll stay here. Fawzi
will summon Nashwa and Aisha. They'll bring you a late
lunch. You'll nourish yourself. Nourish our child. And
when I return, if you still insist on talking, then we'll talk.'

He left after that. As promised, her staff appeared, their
barely suppressed chatter a marked indication that they
were even more excited to be serving her in the Sultan's
private chamber. Their complete lack of judgement as they
darted between the living room and the private kitchen,
where Zaid's personal chef was preparing what sounded
like a feast fit for an army, forced Esme to examine Zaid's
words.

By assuming the throne after his uncle's long tyrannical
rule and giving so much of himself to his people without
asking for anything in return, he'd laid down a path of trust
and dependability and set up the cornerstone for change.

The protests, which had died down in the last few
weeks, were a sign that Zaid was winning even those dis-
gruntled citizens over. She knew through her own studies
and experience with social work that marriage was almost
always a better stability provider than single parenthood.
And when that provider was the ruler of a kingdom…?

Esme believed in her heart she could make it work. But
should the truth ever come out, would Zaid forgive what
she'd done?

By the time she finished sampling a little bit of each
dish set before her, she knew she needed to lay her cards
on the table the moment Zaid returned.

Except, when he walked through the doors five hours
later, a single look was all it took to realise something was
badly wrong.

'I need to leave for Paris immediately,' he announced.

She struggled to her feet, and although he frowned when
she stumbled slightly, he carried on walking towards his

bedroom. Given no choice but to follow or shout the conversation, she trailed behind him.

Two butlers were already packing suitcases, and Zaid was shrugging off his outer robe.

She dragged her gaze from the ripple of muscle beneath his tunic. Already her chest was tightening at the thought of him being absent again much like he'd been for the past ten days. The possible reason for that feeling was a little terrifying but not enough to prevent her from asking, 'Why?'

'A deal I was supposed to finalise at the trade summit next week is in jeopardy. It's been six months in the making. It can't fall apart now.'

Esme wasn't prepared to feel so bereft at the thought of his absence. 'Oh…right. How long will you be away?'

His whole frame brimmed with majestic confidence as he shrugged. 'For as long as it takes to salvage it. I don't intend that to be long at all.'

'Okay. I'll…see you when you get back, then.'

He paused in the process of removing his *keffiyeh*. 'No, you'll see me every day while I'm away because you're coming with me, Esmeralda.'

Her eyes widened. 'I'm… Why?'

His air of determination intensified. 'Because for one thing we haven't finished our conversation. And I'm hoping that once we do agree that marriage is the only course of action, you'll spend the rest of the time consulting with the Royal Palace's designated designers to pick your wedding trousseau.'

A neat, efficiently presented argument. There was no way she could say no unless she was prepared to wait for days, maybe even longer, for Zaid to return from his trip. The thought of having that unfinished conversation hanging over her head, disturbing her sleep, didn't fill her with joy.

'Okay, I'll go and get packed.'

He slanted a very masculine smile her way as he reefed his tunic over his head and headed for his vast dressing room. 'No need. It's being taken care of as we speak.'

It was the sight of his bare torso that robbed her of the heated response she'd planned. Esme was sure of it. Or perhaps the fact that she was still in his bedroom when he re-emerged five minutes later wearing a pair of grey chinos and a pristine white polo shirt.

The casual clothes should have made him less intimidating. Instead, the power of his magnetic attraction seemed to expand even further, encompassing everything in its way. Her included. She watched him glide his fingers hurriedly through his glossy hair and found herself wishing they were hers. Her breath caught when he stopped before her.

'Did you have lunch?' he asked, his face pinched in serious lines.

She nodded, a touch breathlessly, as her senses filled with his scent.

'Good. We should be wheels up in an hour. If you wish to supervise your staff, I suggest you go and do so now.'

Time seemed to trip into fast forward from then. A quick, refreshing shower and a change of clothes into white palazzo linen pants, matching wide-sleeved top and gold wedge sandals, and she was heading out to join Zaid in his motorcade.

The jumbo-sized royal jet, its wings and tail painted in the same signature colours, stood waiting on the tarmac, its crew courteous and efficient as they readied their King for his journey. But, contrary to thinking she would get a chance to speak to Zaid, she was promptly installed in a sumptuous living suite with Nashwa and Aisha keeping her company, while Zaid cloistered himself with his financial advisors in a separate part of the plane.

That theme continued when they reached Paris. Only with more people thrown into the mix. The royal party had hired the whole upper floor of the hotel on Avenue Montaigne, with she and Zaid occupying two separate bedrooms in the Royal Suite. Decorated with typical Parisian glamour, the hotel nevertheless held hints of eastern exoticism that made Esme feel at home the moment she walked in, although the thought that she was beginning to think of Ja'ahr as home struck and stayed with her.

Despite the jaw-dropping elegance of their hotel, Esme felt as if she was on pins and needles as the days rolled by and every opportunity to talk to Zaid was thwarted. In her uncharitable moments, she suspected it was by design. But then she would catch a glimpse of him through an open conference room door, see the haggard expressions of his advisors reflected a hundredfold on his face, and feel regretful. On one of those occasions his gaze caught hers as she hesitated in the doorway. Then his intense eyes dropped to her flat belly for a long moment before he resumed his conversation.

The wordless indication that she and their baby were also on his mind only doubled her guilt.

It was that emotion that stopped her from sending away the designers when they started to arrive on their sixth day in Paris. That and the undeniable fact that her period hadn't made its prompt appearance on her due date. She'd found herself alone with Zaid for a rare minute in the living room a few hours after absorbing that reality.

He'd taken one look at her and frowned. 'What's wrong?'

'I... My period didn't come.'

The brush of knuckles on her cheek was at variance with the almost reproachful look in his eyes as he nodded. 'I know,' was all he said before yet another group of business-suited men walked into the room.

With the confirmation that she was well and truly im-pregnated fixed in her mind, Esme sat in the designated throne-like chair in her suite and watched row after row of exquisite gowns being wheeled into the room.

Apparently, His Highness had requested a full trousseau and new set of clothes for her honeymoon. For the Ja'ahrian wedding, her traditional wedding gown was being prepared in a secret location she wasn't to be privy to.

Esme went through a cycle of frustration, anxiety and anger as she inspected the beautiful gowns. But her mind kept returning to one kernel of hope that wouldn't disap-pear.

Zaid had arranged for all of this despite knowing that her past was less than exemplary. If he was prepared to take a risk for the sake of their child, was she not doing it a disservice by attempting to stand in the way of her child's rightful inheritance?

The only thing holding her back was her secret.

She would tell him. She had to before anything irrevers-ible happened. But in the meantime she squashed down her churning feelings and carried on choosing the clothes that were to her taste.

Nashwa and Aisha's enthusiastic applause the moment she tried the clothes on confirmed her choices. With that out of the way, a knot of anxiety eased and Esme allowed herself to relax a little.

Zaid walked in as the stylists were transporting the clothes to her bedroom. He took one look around, then his eyes zeroed in on her.

'You've chosen your trousseau.' It wasn't a question, but confirmation of what he'd willed her to do all along.

Her breath emerged shakily as she replied. 'Yes.'

'So you will marry me?' This time it was a question, but one he knew the answer to already.

On a silent prayer, Esme swallowed. 'Yes.'

* * *

If she'd thought the events since their arrival in Paris were hurried, the momentum once she'd given her consent was nothing short of warp speed. The morning after, Zaid presented her with a staggeringly beautiful yellow diamond set in Arabian gold. Tears were already prickling her eyes at the sheer beauty of the stone when he informed her solemnly that the ring had belonged to his mother.

The moment would have been perfect, magical even, had it not all been witnessed by his twenty-strong staff and captured on camera by a professional photographer drafted in for the sole purpose of documenting Zaid's formal proposal. After that, a formal announcement was made in Ja'ahr.

Zaid stood in the centre of the room, his hand holding hers, surrounded by his staff as they watched a televised version of the announcement.

The rock of anxiety that sat in her belly doubled in size as the camera panned over the crowds gathered in parks and stadiums to await the news. At the replay of Zaid's proposal, they erupted in deafening cheers.

Inside the hotel suite, his staff also applauded as Zaid leaned down and murmured in her ear, 'I told you they would welcome you with open arms.'

Almost instantly, Esme's popularity exploded.

But then so did the delicate trade talks Zaid had been painstakingly stitching together.

Meetings went on late into the night, tempers frayed and were lost. When he emerged from a conference room three days after their engagement, still looking haggard and frustrated, Esme's heart lurched. Then it dipped even further when he approached her with a grim, resolute look.

'Fawzi is instructing your staff to pack for you. You're returning to Ja'ahr this afternoon.'

It was the last thing she was expecting. The last thing her heart seemed to be prepared for. 'Why?' she blurted, knowing she was in deep trouble where her feelings for Zaid were concerned.

'I'm going to be here for a little longer. And you need to return and ensure the wedding preparations are under way.'

She didn't want to leave, but now she'd agreed to marry him, any objection would be seen as dragging her feet. But there was still an issue between them.

'Zaid, we still need to talk about my past.'

His hand slashed through the air. 'Enough with this need to talk!'

Frustration and anger welled inside her. 'This is important—'

'So is this wedding. Perhaps you ought to concentrate on the future and stop dwelling on the past?' he bit out.

'All I need is ten minutes,' she insisted.

He clawed his fingers through his hair. 'That's ten more than I have right now, Esmeralda. I merely came out here to say goodbye.'

'If all you wanted was to tell me I was being shipped out, perhaps you should've sent Fawzi. Or a text message.'

He growled under his breath. 'I do not wish to fight with you.'

'You don't wish to do anything with me, except throw directives and expect me to jump when you say so!'

His gaze dropped to her stomach. 'In your state, I would prefer less jumping and more co-operation,' he suggested, with a possessive throb in his voice that was directed solely at his heir.

Pain struck somewhere in the region of her heart. 'I'm well aware that I'm merely a vessel for your heir, Zaid, but perhaps you might spare a thought for my state of mind, too?'

He looked puzzled for a moment. That moment passed

almost instantly when Fawzi appeared like an unwanted apparition.

'Your Highness, your presence is needed.'

Zaid exhaled noisily. 'I'll be right there.'

Esme couldn't stop her mouth twisted in bitterness. 'Of course you will.'

His eyes narrowed. 'Esmeralda—'

She waved him away, her gesture carefree despite the pain and anxiety twisting her insides. 'It's fine, Zaid. I understand completely where I stand in the pecking order. So I guess I'll see you when I see you.'

Then she did what he'd done to her many times since their arrival. She left *him* standing there, staring after her.

The return journey to Ja'ahr was uneventful, probably because she retired to the master suite the moment she boarded the jet and spent the whole trip curled up with her pillow for company.

Zaid couldn't have spelled it out more conclusively if he'd tried that she was merely a means to an end. He'd brought her to Paris to apply pressure on her to marry him. The moment she'd agreed her place on the chessboard had become redundant.

And it wasn't as if he'd hidden his motives. Zaid had been upfront about this marriage being for the sole benefit of his people and his heir.

So why did it hurt so much? The answer mocked her in the dull thudding of her heart. Zaid's feelings might be purposefully basic, but along the line hers had gained strings and bows and hopes for a happy ever after with no basis in reality. And even now she feared it was too late.

Melancholy born of that realisation stayed with her long after they landed back in Ja'ahr and into the days that followed. Lost in her gloomy world that not even the joy of the child growing in her womb could shake, it took a while to realise the mood of the people had shifted slightly.

When she started to pay attention, she saw TV reports and debates that questioned her suitability as the daughter of a criminal to be the first lady of Ja'ahr. When further questions arose about her father and her past, her anxiety grew. But then so did her sense of finality. Maybe it was all for the best. Maybe the decision would be taken out of her hands by the people who mattered. Ja'ahr's citizens.

Ironically, her thoughts manifested into reality the very next day, a full week after her return from Paris with almost zero contact from Zaid.

Nashwa's announcement that she had a visitor came as a surprise. An unpleasant one when she realised just who her visitor was.

The chief of police, Ahmed Haruni, was pacing her private office as if he owned the place. Black, beady eyes fixed on her as he lazily replaced the paperweight he'd been examining when Esme entered. Unlike most people did since her betrothal announcement, he didn't bow to her.

Esme didn't care about that as much as she cared to know why he was there. 'Can I help you, sir?'

He didn't leave her hanging for long. 'I'll come straight to the point, Miss Scott. There are a growing number of concerned Ja'ahrians who believe this proposed marriage is a mistake.'

Despite her own growing feelings in that regard, her heart lurched. 'And let me guess, you're one of them?'

The small man shrugged. 'I love my country. It would be remiss of me not to speak up before it's too late.'

'Why are you bringing this to me? Why not take it up with your Sultan?'

He spread his arms wide, a mildly contemptuous look on his face. 'Because he's not here. He's chasing flimsy deals when he should be here, looking after the welfare of his people.'

Anger spiked through her pain. 'The reason for his absence is not flimsy, I assure you.'

'I did not come to debate that with you.'

'Then tell me what you *did* come for.'

His gave a snake-like smile. 'You may have pulled the wool over our leader's eyes, but I know exactly who you are, Miss Scott. I know what happened in Las Vegas with a certain young man named Bryan Atkins.'

Shock lanced through her. He witnessed her reaction and his smile widened. 'Do I have your attention now, Miss Scott?'

She nodded numbly. 'What do you want?'

His eyes hardened. 'For you to do the right thing, of course. If Zaid Al-Ameen isn't fit to rule this country, then *you* are even less fit to be our Sultana.'

She gasped. 'You don't think Zaid is fit to be Sultan?'

'There are others more qualified than he.'

She raised her chin. 'You mean others you can bend to your will?'

Black eyes narrowed. 'You'd be wise to watch your tongue, Miss Scott. The Sultan isn't here to protect you now.'

Icy fingers crawled down her spine. 'Is that all you came to say?'

He reached into his pocket and brought out a rectangular envelope. 'This is a first-class ticket back to your country. I will be pleased to provide you with a police escort to the airport if you wish it.'

'I don't wish it, thank you. *If* I decide to leave, I'll do so under my own steam.'

He placed the envelope on her desk anyway and walked towards her. Esme fought the urge to step back from his oily, menacing presence. 'Get out of the country while you still have the chance, Miss Scott. This regime will not thrive for much longer.'

With that ominous threat, he walked out.

Esme expelled the breath she'd been holding, then immediately gulped in another. Her mind darted back and forth, debating which action to take first. She needed to warn Zaid. But she also needed to put into action the thoughts she'd been skirting before the chief of police's noxious visit.

She couldn't marry Zaid.

Not now she knew the depths of her feelings for him. Not now she knew her presence would cause nothing but dissension among his people.

The walk to her desk felt like a walk to the gallows. But surprisingly the letter was easy to compose. As was the packing of her things three hours later. She thought of calling her father but discarded the idea. His phone calls were being monitored, and the last thing she needed was for her quiet exit to be announced. But what surprised her most was how easy her request to be driven to the airport was granted.

The ticket attendant smiled widely and nodded when she requested a seat on the next available flight out of Ja'ahr. Esme didn't care that it was headed to Rome instead of England. It was close enough.

It was only as she began the two-hour wait for her flight that Esme got an inkling that something was going on. First the attendant came to inform her that her flight was delayed for a further two hours. Then the area around where she sat slowly started to empty of people. When she realised they were being herded away from her, Esme looked around and caught a few phone cameras pointed her way. Next she realised the bodyguards she thought she'd dismissed were still very much present. And a few more were fanned out close by.

Esme rose from her seat as a hum built in the gathering crowd. When someone pointed at the window behind her, she turned. And swallowed hard at the sight of the royal jet parked on the tarmac.

In the next instant she saw Zaid, robes flowing, ruthless intent stamped on his face as he stalked towards her.

When he reached her he said nothing. Not with his lips anyway. His eyes however, blazed with fury, censure and disappointment.

'Zaid—'

'We are in public, *jamila*, and that is the only thing saving you from being placed over my knee and spanked to within an inch of your life,' he growled, nostrils flared. 'Now you will smile and take my hand and we will walk out of here and return to the palace.'

Her heart leapt wildly. Then plummeted just as hard.

'I can't.'

The tendons in his neck stood out as he struggled to control himself. 'You can and you will. I'm not letting you go, Esmeralda.'

'But, Zaid, the chief of police—'

'Has been thoroughly and conclusively dealt with.' He held up the letter she'd written to him, his eyes as cold as chips, although she caught something in there too. Something that made her heart lurch wildly. 'This changes nothing, Esmeralda. You're not leaving me. This wedding is going to happen, so get used to the idea.'

CHAPTER THIRTEEN

THE JA'AHRIAN MARRIAGE ceremony was like nothing she'd ever witnessed. Celebrated over a seven-day period, each evening at sunset, she and Zaid met before a different set of marriage elders to repeat vows of faithfulness, honour and devotion, after which they hosted a banquet for the thousand-strong guests and dignitaries who'd accepted their invitation.

Had she been in a different state of mind, sheer awe would have rolled through her, each moment steeped in vivid Technicolor. But the pain and bewilderment lodged in her heart made names and faces blur into one, even as she pasted on a fake smile until she was sure her face would split in two.

She was gazing entranced at fireworks that marked the official end to the celebrations when she felt Zaid's eyes on her.

His refusal to accept her backing out of the wedding had been absolute, his fury at her going back on her word catastrophic.

Esme would have fought and rejected both had she not realised, at the moment she'd seen him walking towards her at the airport, that she was irrevocably, for better or worse, requited or not, head over heels in love with Zaid Al-Ameen.

He'd made the right decision. His wife, his Queen, and the future mother of his children was beautiful, poised, and a natural with his people. Many had come to the gates of the palace to offer her flowers. After the ceremony, before they departed for their honeymoon, she would take her place next to his and thank his people for their support in a live broadcast.

All this could easily not have come to pass. He should have acted sooner to deal with Ahmed Haruni but he'd needed that final piece of evidence that the man had been inciting others to overthrow Zaid's rule. He could so easily have lost Esmeralda. The knowledge still had the power to shake him. Even now, watching her, he knew how close it had all been.

But no matter. They were married now. And Zaid couldn't wait to show her off to the world. More than that, he couldn't wait to be alone with her. To reacquaint himself with the delights of her body. And then perhaps the infernal hunger that dogged him would ease. He mentally shrugged. But who cared if it didn't? She was his wife. His partner in life. They would always have each other.

So why did he feel a kernel of unease gnawing at him each time he saw a shadow cross her face?

He shook off the bad feeling. The doctor had declared her healthy and strong, her pregnancy thriving. And if the feelings swirling through him grew into something else…why not?

He firmly broke off the conversation with the talkative minister and returned to his wife's side. Taking her hand, he pressed a kiss to the back of it, grimacing inwardly when he felt her stiffen slightly. His behaviour at the airport had left a lot to be desired, he knew. But he intended to work on it. 'It's time to say our goodbyes.'

Her eyes widened. 'Already?'

'They've had seven days of you. It's my turn to spend time *alone* with you.'

He made sure their goodbyes were quick, and the prepared speech was gratifying but brief.

Then, finally done, he instructed his driver to deliver them to his jet. It was time to make Esmeralda his wife in every sense of the word.

* * *

They flew to the Bahamas before boarding the royal yacht moored in Nassau. Although travelling in extreme luxury had its perks, Esme was still tired when they finally arrived on board. Turned out keeping her emotions under constant guard did that to a woman. She may have admitted her feelings to herself, but she didn't intend to admit them to Zaid. Not when it was clear he wouldn't welcome them.

They set sail immediately, the idea being to island-hop for the next two weeks.

Nashwa and Aisha had remained behind this time, and although Esme found herself missing their effervescent presence, she welcomed the peace and quiet and the chance to bathe and clothe herself without their well-intentioned interference.

She was still fighting the emotions that seemed to bubble just below her skin when the door to the opulent shower cubicle opened and a very naked and aroused Zaid stepped in.

She had a mere second to school her features, but the weeks since they had first made love had done nothing but sharpen the edge of her desire, and by the time he prowled over to where the water cascaded over her body, every atom of her being was on fire for him.

'Is it irrational that I am jealous of the water caressing your body?' he enquired huskily as he lowered his head to trail a kiss across one shoulder.

She jerked back, bumped her shoulder on the wall. 'What...what are you doing in here?'

His eyes narrowed. 'If you have to ask then something's seriously wrong.' He prowled closer.

She had nowhere to go, so she held out a warding hand. 'I know we're on our honeymoon, but...'

'But?'

'I... Zaid, you don't really want me—'

'Take a very good look, *habiba*. The evidence speaks for itself, I believe.'

Her hungry gaze swept over him, her face flaming when it lingered on the proud, rigid parts of his anatomy.

'I...don't mean that.'

He sighed. 'We got off to a rocky start, I admit. But whatever problems we need to iron out, let's not make this one of them. Okay?'

She knew she was weak when it came to him. Esme discovered just how weak when her body, independent of her mind, lunged into his arms.

He made a rough sound in his throat, then took her mouth in a hot, carnal, demanding kiss. Like the first and second time, he set her aflame with just his mouth. But now she knew what else was coming. And she could barely contain herself. Boldly, she caressed him, driving him to the same fever pitch he'd inspired in her.

On a wild whim, she grabbed the gel she'd just used, squeezing a few drops into her palm. The moment he broke the kiss, she stepped back and glided her hands over his torso. The surprise on his face was followed instantaneously by encouragement. Hard on the heels of that came a rough, thick curse before he was bundling her out of the shower and drying them off.

When they reached the bed, he lifted her high, his gaze upturned to hers. 'Now I truly make you my wife.'

'And you my husband.'

The arms that laid her reverently on the bed shook a little. The kiss he bestowed on her lacked a little of his usual smooth finesse. But she didn't care.

The magnificent man she'd fallen in love with was making love to her. Yes, there was pain in her heart, but for now there was bliss too. And she intended to hold onto that for as long as possible.

That was her last thought before Zaid kissed his way

down her body. Before he lingered on the flat plane of her belly where their child grew.

Before, after praising her through her first climax, he rose above her and took her body with his.

Unhurried, exquisite, their union brought tears to her eyes and a gruff shout from Zaid when he reached his own peak. Then, arms wrapped around each other, they slid into sleep.

It set the tone for their honeymoon.

By day they ate, sunbathed and explored the islands. And by night they made love after sharing mouth-watering meals on the top deck and talking long into the night.

Besides his bodyguards, only Fawzi and another member of his staff accompanied them. Their presence barely registered, although Fawzi had taken to bowing from the waist when he walked into her presence.

When she commented on it, Zaid laughed.

'And why does he look disconcerted whenever I speak to him?'

'Because he's there solely for my benefit. And also because he sees it as a sign of disrespect to me to be brought into a private conversation.'

'But I mean no disrespect! Surely he knows that?'

'Whether you do or not doesn't alter his belief.'

'Really?'

Zaid sobered. 'Yes. There was a time when he would've been severely punished for being addressed directly in the presence of his ruler.'

'What? That's preposterous! It's not his fault if he's spoken to while he's in the room.'

'He's supposed to be unobtrusive. Being made to feel self-conscious doesn't sit right with him.'

'Okay. Thanks for telling me that. I'll make sure he's not uncomfortable in my presence.'

She gasped when he caught her hand and linked their

fingers. 'You're a true gem, Esmeralda Al-Ameen. I'm a very blessed man.'

Esme allowed her heart to take the leap it wanted. Although it soon fell with the knowledge that with each day that passed, and the more she fell under her husband's spell, the more heartache she was inviting.

As for her rush to tell Zaid her sordid secret, he'd said her past didn't matter. She'd decided to take his word for it.

For now.

One day he would need to know. And when that day came, she would tell him.

Except the day came much, much sooner than she anticipated. Eleven days into their two-week honeymoon, to be exact. It didn't matter that the day was perfect, cloudless and the happiest day of her life.

The moment Fawzi walked onto the sunny middle deck, where she and Zaid were having post-swimming drinks, she knew her days in paradise were over. His bow to her was brusque, and when he spoke it wasn't in the deferential English he'd taken to speaking to both of them but in his master's language.

Slowly, she watched Zaid's whole body turn deathly still, then he started to fire questions at his private secretary. Questions Fawzi answered without once looking her way. But Zaid was looking straight at her, with cold eyes that froze her to the marrow. He spoke again to his assistant, and this time Fawzi's gaze darted to her. Esme wished he'd kept ignoring her. That way she wouldn't have seen the pity in his eyes.

He started to walk away. Zaid issued one last instruction. The younger man actually swallowed before he bowed and left the deck.

Thick silence ensued. Despite the blazing temperatures, she shivered.

'You know about Bryan, don't you?' Her voice was as weak as she felt.

His nostrils flared for a wild instant before he spoke. 'Is it true? He killed himself because you fleeced him out of one hundred thousand dollars then rejected him?'

Her heart shook with misery. 'No, it was my father. But he wouldn't have gone after Bryan if I hadn't made friends with him. My interest in him was what triggered my father's attention.' Like every time she thought about Bryan, she wished she'd walked away the day he'd approached her in that restaurant in Vegas.

'This is the guy who took you in his helicopter?' he pressed. 'He's the reason you're racked with guilt whenever you approach a helicopter?'

She nodded, her throat clogged with a boulder of dreadful pain. Not just because of the memory but the certain knowledge that she was about to lose Zaid.

'When did he take his own life?'

'The day after I refused his proposal. It was a few days before my eighteenth birthday. He wanted us to get married on my birthday. I said no. I was too young. God, so was he. We rowed after the helicopter ride and I never saw him again. A few days later his letter arrived. My father had emptied his bank account. Bryan thought I'd helped Dad to do it, but I didn't. I hadn't known anything about it. I tried to get my father to return the money. But...'

'But?' Zaid demanded harshly.

'It was too late. Bryan threw himself off a bridge that morning.'

His face hardened. 'Did you know he loved you? Did *you* love him?'

'No, I didn't love him. He was just my friend. But I love you, Zaid,' she confessed desperately.

Wrong time. Wrong place. She knew it before his head

went back and his eyes went black as if her words had physically assaulted him.

'You *love* me? What a curious time to admit it. Do you think it'll distract me from the fact that this news could rip apart the fragile foundations I've built in Ja'ahr?'

The tears choking her finally fell free. 'I didn't say it because of that. I said it because it's true.' She stopped, her heart bleeding. 'I'm sorry.'

He rose from the lounger and paced away from her. 'Sorry? A man lost his life because of your father's greed! Several newspapers are poised to print that you and your father lured him in with lies and falsehoods, knowing all the time he was nothing but a pawn to you. My people have fallen in love with you. *I…*' he stopped and gritted his jaw.

Her heart shredded into a tiny million pieces. She pulled her knees to her chest, wrapped her arms around her cold body. 'I promise I didn't know about what my father did to Bryan, Zaid, not until it was too late. But I should have known what my father was up to. I blame myself for bringing Bryan into my life.'

When he didn't say anything, she ventured a glance. His face was an ashen landscape of anger and condemnation.

'I've tried to become a better person. By doing whatever good I can wherever I can,' she pleaded.

But he was gone.

He may have been physically on the deck with her but she'd lost her husband. The man she really shouldn't have married in the first place. And when he turned and walked away without uttering another word to her, all she could do was bury her face in her arms and sob her heart out.

Needless to say, the honeymoon was over. Within a few hours the yacht was back in its moorings, their bags were packed and they were headed towards Nassau airport.

At first she was confused by the sight of two identical

planes on the tarmac. When the penny dropped, her already shredded heart dropped along with it.

'I'm going home alone, aren't I?' she asked Zaid the moment he stepped out of the SUV.

'Yes, it's for the best.'

The harsh laughter that escaped scraped her throat. 'Is it?' she asked, mostly self-mockingly.

To her surprise, he nodded. 'It's best if we don't travel together.'

'But why?'

'It's protocol when you're carrying my future heir. We shouldn't have travelled here together.'

'Then why did we?'

'I needed... I chose to bend the rules a little.'

'And now you're back to being Mr Responsible?'

His jaw flexed. 'Your crew is waiting, Esmeralda. And I need to do what I can to prevent this from ruining everything.' He strode off and boarded the first aircraft.

And when the pilot of the second jet summoned her, she walked with leaden legs, boarded the plane and flew to Ja'ahr alone.

Only to find out on her arrival at the palace that Zaid wasn't in residence. According to the staff left manning his office when she visited each morning, they had no clue when His Highness would be available.

Esme discovered very quickly that she was being held prisoner in her own palace. Without Zaid she had no authorisation to leave the palace grounds, not even with an armed escort. But she discovered that whatever damage control he was exerting seemed to be working. At least on an international level. No news outlet carried the story.

But within Ja'ahr, protests that had started to die down rose up again, with one in particular staged close to the palace gates.

Three weeks after her return, she was standing at the

viewing window that circled the palace's giant dome when Nashwa approached her.

'Am I imagining it or has the crowd grown since yesterday?' Esme asked worriedly.

'You're not imagining it, Your Highness. Those are Ahmed Haruni's people, protesting his arrest.'

She winced at the title, her heart tearing as it did each time she heard the reminder of who she was now.

She also knew that on some level Ahmed Haruni had spoken the truth. She would never be completely accepted here.

After a minute of watching the group of angry youths waving their placards, she turned to Nashwa. 'I'm sorry. Did you want something?'

'No, Your Highness. But there's someone here to see you.'

Her heart leapt for a wild minute, then she mocked herself for her foolishness. If Zaid had returned the whole palace would have been abuzz by now. It wouldn't be the soulless place it felt like now.

That too was her fault.

She swallowed her sigh and followed Nashwa down to the office she'd been designated but had never used as Sultana. The man waiting for her was vaguely familiar. He came forward and offered a shallow bow.

'Forgive the intrusion, Your Highness. My name is Anwar Hanuf, a surrogate uncle to His Highness.'

Esme nodded. 'Yes, you're one of his advisors. I remember you from the wedding.'

He smiled. 'It's kind of you to recall our brief meeting.'

Nodding again, she indicated a chair. 'What can I do for you?' she said after they'd sat down and he'd declined refreshments.

'I'm afraid I'm going to be blunt.'

Her stomach dipped but she kept her composure. 'I can do blunt.'

'You've seen the crowd gathered outside the palace gate, I'm sure.'

'Yes, I have.'

'In my experience situations like this only escalate unless they're dealt with.'

'I would gladly talk to them, but sadly I've been forbidden from leaving the palace.'

He nodded. 'For your safety and that of our future ruler, that is the right decision.'

'Is it? Only I would've liked to have been consulted before those decisions were made regarding my safety. Sadly, my husband seems to have fallen off the face of the earth.'

A look crossed his face and her breath caught. 'You know where Zaid is, don't you?'

'That is not why I'm here—'

'Is he planning on coming back here anytime soon?' she blurted.

He sighed. 'It's time to do the right thing, Miss Scott.'

She wanted to tell him her name was Esme Al-Ameen, but the cold tingling at her nape pushed the words back down.

'The people's hearts and their trust have been broken. You need to cauterise the wounds so they can heal. Or we'll only be going backwards.'

'What exactly are you asking of me?'

He stared fixedly at her. 'I think you know.' He rose and bowed. 'Good day to you, Miss Scott.'

Sorrow scraped at her insides as her heart dropped to her feet. Two emissaries, bearing the same message. She couldn't bury her head in the sand any more. She placed the calls she needed to make, then dialled the number of the palace security team.

'This is Sultana Al-Ameen. I'm expecting guests at

the palace gates within the hour. Make sure they're admitted and shown every courtesy, then let me know when they're ready.'

'Yes, Your Highness.'

She put the phone down, feeling like a complete fraud. But she reassured herself that she'd never have to use her power and title again.

The vans started to arrive after half an hour.

When the call came, she rose and headed to the conference room. Lights mounted on powerful cameras and TV lenses erupted when she entered the room, and for the first time, she was glad of the bodyguards standing on alert nearby.

Tears threatened again but she swallowed hard and unfolded her piece of paper.

'Thank you for coming. And thank you to every single Ja'ahrian who has made me feel welcome since my arrival. I've fallen in love with this beautiful country and been proud to call it my home.' She cleared her throat. 'But I also realise that I've been very unfair to you. My father's and my less than stellar pasts should not be the burden of the people. My mistakes should not be the cause of your unhappiness. So from this moment, I renounce my position as your Sultana. I should not have taken the position in the first place, not without baring my heart and showing you the whole truth. But I hope you will still accept your Sultan's child when he or she is born. Our baby is innocent in all this. Please don't let him or her pay for my mistakes. The same goes for your Sultan, Zaid Al-Ameen. He deserves better than me. But most of all he deserves your love, your respect and your understanding. I leave him in your tender care. *Shukraan*, Ja'ahr.'

She stepped off the podium and let the bodyguards steer her away from the barrage of questions that exploded through the room. She managed to hold it together until she was safely behind closed doors. Then she hugged her arms around her body and sobbed. When there were no more tears left, she trudged to her dressing room. She was folding her black dress into the small pile on the centre island when a white-faced Nashwa rushed in.

Esme smiled sadly. 'Can you find a suitcase for me? I can't seem to find one anywhere. An overnight bag will do.' She'd never got round to giving up her flat in London. She could slot back into being Esme Scott as if she'd never left.

'But...where are you going, Your Highness?' Nashwa shrieked. 'And what you said on the TV...'

'I'm sorry you had to find out that way. But I really need the bag. Please?'

Nashwa stared at her for long seconds before she plugged her fist in her mouth and fled the room. On automatic, Esme resumed gathering her things. Half an hour later, when it was clear Nashwa wasn't going to return, Esme looked through her shelves and took down the biggest handbag she could find. She was stuffing the meagre belongings into it when the bedroom door slammed back on its hinges.

A moment later, Zaid stood framed in the door of her dressing room.

'What did you do, *habiba*?' he breathed raggedly. 'What the *hell* did you do?'

The sight of him. Oh, God. He looked terrible, thick stubble bracing his jaw. He'd suffered. Because of her. And still she trembled from head to toe with the purely selfish need to rush into his arms, clasp herself to his wonderful strength. But she held herself still. 'It was the right thing to do,' she murmured.

Fists clenched tight, he crossed the room in five quick strides. 'No, it wasn't, you fool! Are you going to try and leave me every time my back is turned?'

'Don't shout at me. Not after pulling another disappearing act on me.'

He took another step closer, bringing his bristling, glorious body within touching distance. 'I'll do whatever I want when you act like...like...' He clawed a hand through his hair. 'Like the noblest sacrificial lamb to an undeserving bastard.'

Her mouth dropped open. 'What?'

'What you said on TV was—'

'All true.'

He cupped her jaw oh-so-gently. 'No, *jamila*, not all true. What happened was unfortunate and wrong. But your father was the one who took his money. Not you. You were still a child, caught on the end of her father's puppet strings. A father who, I'm guessing, liked to dangle the threat of leaving you very often?'

Pain ripped through her as she nodded. 'I only spent the school holidays with him but even then he threatened me with foster care if I didn't toe his line.'

'And the fear of losing what is right in front of you is even worse than missing what you no longer have, isn't it?'

'Yes. So much more.' Her voice broke and a sob ripped free.

His thumbs caressed her cheeks. 'Shh, *habiba*. Don't cry. It pains me to see your tears.'

'Why? You walked away from me. You were furious with me.'

'Yes, but I was never far away from you. I can never be. I started off being angry with you because a loss of life is personal to me. I also lost sight of the fact that I was a child once too. I know what the pain of losing a parent feels like. After losing your mother, you lived in constant threat of losing your remaining parent, even if you'd have been better off without him.'

She nodded. 'One time, when I was sixteen, I woke up

one morning in our hotel, and Jeffrey was gone. No note, nothing. I'd refused to help him land a mark the night before. He was livid. I was in a strange country and terrified. He capitalised on that. I promised myself the moment I turned eighteen that I would walk away from him. I wish I'd stayed away from Bryan too.'

He nodded, his face set. 'I know. But there's something you don't know. I had Atkins investigated.'

She frowned. 'And?'

'He suffered from severe depression and had attempted suicide more than once.'

Her heart squeezed. 'That doesn't make it any better.'

'No, but he went to Vegas with the aim of blowing all his inheritance and then ending his life that weekend.'

'Oh, God.'

'It's cold comfort, I know, *habiba*, but his mind was made up. But you have people who need you, who love you. Do you know that since your press conference there's been an online petition for you to stay?'

'What?'

'If you renounce your title I'll renounce mine too.'

She gasped. 'You can't. Your people need you. Anwar said—'

'To hell with what Anwar said. He thinks he was acting in my best interests. I'll talk to him later. And anyone else who thinks they know my heart. The only thing they need to know is that it won't beat without you. So where you go, I go.'

'No, Zaid, you're better off—'

'Without my heart? Without my soul? Without the very air I need to live? No, *jamila*. I might as well be dead then.'

'Oh, Zaid...'

His fingers slid into her hair, and he leaned down to brush her lips with his. 'I was going to tell you I loved you that afternoon on the deck. You know that?'

Her gasp whispered over his lips. 'You love me?'

'Oh, yes, my love. So very much. Fawzi couldn't have picked a worse time to deliver his news. I think it's partly why I behaved like a wounded bear. I'm sorry, Esmeralda. Can you forgive me?'

'I forgive you, because I love you too. I managed to tell you, though, remember?'

He grimaced, although his face transformed at her confession. 'I remember, and I'm ashamed to have rejected it then. I would be honoured if you would tell me again.'

'I love you, Zaid Al-Ameen.'

He sealed her lips in a kiss that lifted her heart and her soul. Her heart grew bigger when his hand dropped to caress her belly. 'And you'll remain the wife of my heart? The mother of this beautiful blessing bestowed on us and the many more to come?'

'Yes, Zaid.'

He exhaled shakily, kissed her one more time, before sweeping her off her feet.

A long while later, they lay, blissful, content and gloriously naked on her bed.

With a smile, she caressed his hard chest. 'So did I cause a lot of trouble renouncing my title?'

He chuckled richly. 'It takes a hell of a lot more than a speech to give me up, *habiba*. But attempt it again and I will have you jump through a lifetime of hoops. Even then you won't be free.'

'And why not?'

He rolled her over in one smooth move and braced her hands above her head. 'Because Al-Ameens marry for life. I'm never letting you go. Not even in the afterlife,' he growled.

She leaned up and kissed his beautiful mouth, her heart brimming with happiness. 'That's good, because your Sultana is happy exactly where she is. By your side. For ever.'

EPILOGUE

One year later

'ARE YOU GOING to re-create our honeymoon *exactly* the way it happened last year?' Esme laughed as her husband rolled towards her and trailed a kiss over her shoulder.

'Right up to the point where I ruined it, yes. And then I intend to make it all better from then on. I want the memory erased from your mind for ever.'

'It's already better for me, Zaid. I promise,' she murmured, gliding her fingers through his thick black hair when he levered himself over her.

He placed a lingering kiss on her lips before he raised his head. 'Shhh, don't spoil my plans.' He glanced at his phone nearby. 'It's almost three fifteen. One more minute,' he murmured.

Esme's eyebrows rose. 'You remember the exact time?'

'It was supposed to be a momentous occasion, *jamila*. It's imprinted in my memory.'

The phone beeped softly. Zaid's gaze shifted from it to her face, his features settling into the same mask of love and devotion she'd witnessed so many times in the past year.

'I love you, Esmeralda. So much more than I ever thought I could love anyone. I thank Allah every day that he brought you to me. That you found space in your heart for me. Everything that I am is devoted to you. I will love you even after the breath leaves my body.'

'Oh, Zaid... I love you, too. So much it hurts sometimes.'

He lowered his head and they sealed their love with a

kiss. Then he raised his head and elevated a brow. 'So, are you happy you stayed?'

She laughed. 'Ecstatic. Not that I had a choice after my renunciation of my title was so thoroughly rejected.'

They both laughed, then her joy dimmed a little.

Zaid caressed a thumb down her cheek. 'You're thinking about your father again.'

She nodded. 'Being a mother myself now, feeling the way I do about Amir, it hurts to think that I was so unlovable that he couldn't—'

'No, *habiba*. It wasn't you who was unlovable. It was your father. Not everyone is cut out to be a father. He failed in his duty to you and to your mother. You have nothing to blame yourself for.'

Although she nodded, her heart shook with sadness as she thought of all the opportunities she would never have.

Jeffrey Scott's death in prison from a heart attack two months into his eight-year prison sentence had come as a shock. Despite everything, Esme mourned the fact that they would never have a normal loving relationship and that he'd never get to meet her beloved son, Amir. But that too was something she would eventually put behind her.

Especially when she had more love than she could ever dream of from the husband of her wildest dreams and the son who made her heart burst with gratitude and joy every day.

As if summoned, Aisha mounted the steps to the deck with her precious bundle cradled in her arms.

'Ah, a much better interruption this time round,' Zaid observed with immense satisfaction. 'Although I was hoping to follow that declaration of love with a very physical demonstration.'

Esme smiled and dropped a kiss on his mouth. 'You'll get your chance later, I promise.'

'I'll hold you to that,' he drawled. Then sat up to hold out his arms for his son.

She watched him cradle their son in his strong arms, his face a picture of utter bliss. And then, just because she couldn't help herself, Esme rose too, and put her arms around both her men.

The man of her heart glanced up and smiled, deep abiding love blazing in eyes. 'I love you, Esmeralda.'

The last of her sadness evaporated. 'I love you, too, my Sultan.'

In the brilliant sunlight, the son of her soul gurgled happily as he watched his parents seal their love with one more kiss.

* * * * *

If you enjoyed
THE SULTAN DEMANDS HIS HEIR
why not explore these other stories
by Maya Blake?

PREGNANT AT ACOSTA'S DEMAND
A DEAL WITH ALEJANDRO
ONE NIGHT WITH GAEL

Available now!

MILLS & BOON®
Hardback – November 2017

ROMANCE

The Italian's Christmas Secret	Sharon Kendrick
A Diamond for the Sheikh's Mistress	Abby Green
The Sultan Demands His Heir	Maya Blake
Claiming His Scandalous Love-Child	Julia James
Valdez's Bartered Bride	Rachael Thomas
The Greek's Forbidden Princess	Annie West
Kidnapped for the Tycoon's Baby	Louise Fuller
A Night, A Consequence, A Vow	Angela Bissell
Christmas with Her Millionaire Boss	Barbara Wallace
Snowbound with an Heiress	Jennifer Faye
Newborn Under the Christmas Tree	Sophie Pembroke
His Mistletoe Proposal	Christy McKellen
The Spanish Duke's Holiday Proposal	Robin Gianna
The Rescue Doc's Christmas Miracle	Amalie Berlin
Christmas with Her Daredevil Doc	Kate Hardy
Their Pregnancy Gift	Kate Hardy
A Family Made at Christmas	Scarlet Wilson
Their Mistletoe Baby	Karin Baine
The Texan Takes a Wife	Charlene Sands
Twins for the Billionaire	Sarah M. Anderson

MILLS & BOON®
Large Print – November 2017

ROMANCE

HISTORICAL

MEDICAL

MILLS & BOON®
Hardback – December 2017

ROMANCE

His Queen by Desert Decree	Lynne Graham
A Christmas Bride for the King	Abby Green
Captive for the Sheikh's Pleasure	Carol Marinelli
Legacy of His Revenge	Cathy Williams
A Night of Royal Consequences	Susan Stephens
Carrying His Scandalous Heir	Julia James
Christmas at the Tycoon's Command	Jennifer Hayward
Innocent in the Billionaire's Bed	Clare Connelly
Snowed in with the Reluctant Tycoon	Nina Singh
The Magnate's Holiday Proposal	Rebecca Winters
The Billionaire's Christmas Baby	Marion Lennox
Christmas Bride for the Boss	Kate Hardy
Christmas with the Best Man	Susan Carlisle
Navy Doc on Her Christmas List	Amy Ruttan
Christmas Bride for the Sheikh	Carol Marinelli
Her Knight Under the Mistletoe	Annie O'Neil
The Nurse's Special Delivery	Louisa George
Her New Year Baby Surprise	Sue MacKay
His Secret Son	Brenda Jackson
Best Man Under the Mistletoe	Jules Bennett